Retold Myths & Folktales

African Myths

African American Folktales

Asian Myths

Classic Myths, Volume 1

Classic Myths, Volume 2

Classic Myths, Volume 3

Mexican American Folktales

Native American Myths

Northern European Myths

World Myths

The Retold Tales® Series features novels, short story anthologies, and collections of myths and folktales.

Perfection Learning®

Contributing Writers

Wim Coleman
M.A.T. English and Education
Educational writer and novelist

Pat Perrin
Ph.D. Art Theory and Criticism
Educational writer and novelist

Northern European *Myths*

Perfection Learning®

Senior Editor
Marsha James

Inside Illustration
Don Tate

Editor
Terry Ofner

Book Design
Dea Marks

Cover Illustration
Mark Bischel

For information contact
Perfection Learning® Corporation
1000 North Second Avenue, P.O. Box 500
Logan, Iowa 51546-0500
Phone: 1-800-831-4190 • Fax: 1-800-543-2745
perfectionlearning.com

Paperback ISBN 1-5631-2262-6
Cover Craft® ISBN 0-7807-1702-3

TABLE
OF CONTENTS

WELCOME TO THE RETOLD NORTHERN EUROPEAN MYTHS

The world you are about to enter is an extraordinary one. It is a cold, dark, and mist-filled place where warriors, both male and female, wander in search of adventure. In this world wizards change shape at will, and dragons and dwarfs fight over hordes of gold. This is the world of Northern European mythology.

The eight stories retold here represent the people and folkways of Northern Europe—a region that includes Iceland to the east, Norway and Sweden to the north, and Germany, England, and Ireland to the south. Most of these myths were first written down during the Middle Ages (A.D. 400 to 1400). But the stories were part of an oral tradition that reaches back to the original tribes and peoples that inhabited Europe.

On the whole, the mythology of Northern Europe is heavy and dark. Heroes, such as the Anglo-Saxon Beowulf and the British King Arthur, meet their end. Even gods and whole ways of life pass away. But these heroes and gods of the North don't go quietly. They face death proudly, knowing that their brave deeds will earn them everlasting glory in the songs of poets and story-tellers.

By reading these tales, you bring those old songs back to life. Imagine that the cold wind is at the door. A warm fire snaps in the hearth. Then listen as the minstrel brings news of the deeds of the men and women of the North.

RETOLD UPDATE

This book presents a collection of eight adapted myths from Northern Europe. All the variety, excitement, and humorous details of the original versions are here. But dated language has been "translated" into more current and readable prose.

In addition, a word list has been added at the beginning of each story. Each word defined on that list is printed in dark type within the story. If you forget the meaning of one of these words, just check the list to review the definition.

You'll also find footnotes at the bottom of some story pages. These notes identify people or places, explain ideas, show pronunciations, or provide cultural information.

We offer two other features you may wish to use. One is a map of Northern Europe on page one. This map locates the region where each of the myths was first told.

You will find more cultural information in the Insights section after each myth. These revealing and sometimes amusing facts will give you insight into Northern European cultures, the tellers of the myths, or related myths.

One last word. Since many of the these myths have been retold often, many versions exist. So a story you read here may differ from a version you read elsewhere.

Now on to the myths. We hope you discover the mystery and adventure of these stories from Northern Europe.

MAP OF NORTHERN EUROPE
(A.D. 400 - 1400)

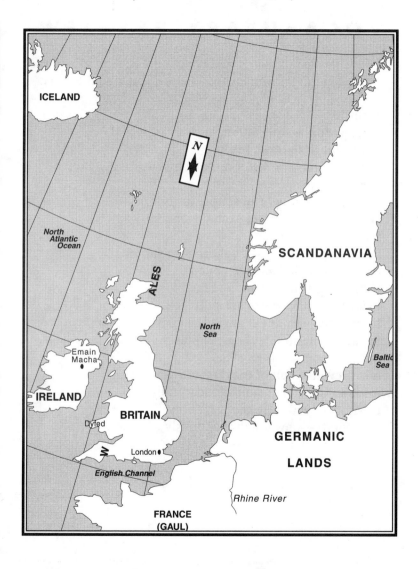

SIR GAWAIN AND THE GREEN KNIGHT

VOCABULARY PREVIEW

Below is a list of words that appear in the story. Read the list and get to know the words before you read the story.

absurdity—foolishness; nonsense
anticipation—expectation
boisterous—spirited; lively
compliments—words of respect; praises
conjurer—magician; wizard
discretion—thoughtful action; caution
embodiment—perfect example; model
fate—destiny; future
fellowship—a group of equals; association
flinched—pulled back; recoiled
gallant—courteous; noble; brave
hearty—strong; warm; friendly
hospitality—kindness towards a guest; politeness
instincts—natural feelings; impulses
lust—desire; craving
mischievous—full of trickery; playful
mockingly—full of ridicule; scornfully
modestly—with meekness; humbly
reluctantly—unwillingly; cautiously
virtue—purity; goodness

Main Characters

King Arthur—King of Britain
Sir Gawain—King Arthur's nephew; most honorable
  knight of the Round Table
Green Knight—stranger who visits King Arthur's court
Lord and his wife—Sir Gawain's hosts
Morgan le Fay—magician; King Arthur's half sister

The Scene

The story begins at Camelot, King Arthur's legendary kingdom in England. Then action moves to another castle somewhere in northern England. Finally the story ends in the Green Chapel.

Sir Gawain and the Green Knight

Sir Gawain was the most famous knight of Camelot. He was gallant, honest, generous, and virtuous. But he had one more lesson to learn. And the dreadful and mysterious Green Knight was just the one to teach him.

What thrilling tale of adventure and conquest will it be this year?" King Arthur asked himself. "What marvelous feat of arms[1] will be told to bring wonder and joy to this New Year's Eve feast?"

King Arthur stood at the head table of the banquet hall. Gaily colored banners hung all around. One hundred fifty knights and their ladies were seated at tables in the great hall. All the knights of King Arthur's Round Table[2] had been celebrating the Christmas season for fifteen days now.

Holiday cheer had echoed through the halls of the castle Camelot.[3] The guests had laughed by day and danced by night—sharing more food and merriment than anyone could imagine. The knights had offered fine gifts to one another and to their ladies. The ladies dressed in their finest gowns and wore green garlands in their hair.

---

[1] A feat of arms is a noble military action that requires strength, courage, and skill.

[2] King Arthur's Round Table was a legendary table around which all the knights sat when making decisions. At the table all knights shared power equally.

[3] Camelot is a legendary place. Camelot was the name of King Arthur's favorite castle and the city surrounding it. Even in legend, Camelot was not the capital of Britain. London was, as it is today.

Tonight's feast would mark the end of the festivities.

"These knights are the finest and most **gallant** gentlemen in the world," thought Arthur. "Certainly one among them will tell of some wonder or miracle he has witnessed."

You see, Arthur followed the same custom every year. He wouldn't sit down to eat the New Year's Eve feast until one of his knights told a story of chivalry.[4] So he stood straight and proud—waiting.

Arthur was a young king at the height of his power and fame. He was the ruler of all Britain, and his name was known throughout Europe. Seated at Arthur's right was his beautiful wife, Guinevere[5]—a worthy queen to the world's most powerful ruler. To Guinevere's right were Arthur's brave nephews—Sir Agravain[6] and his brother Sir Gawain.[7] Sir Gawain was famous for his courage and courtesy.

A blast of trumpets announced the first course of dinner. Servants came, placing silver dishes filled with meats and sweets upon the table. Soon the tables became so full that there was nowhere to put another platter. Pipes and drums played **boisterous** melodies as everyone ate and drank and laughed. Everyone but Arthur, that is. He was still waiting for a tale.

"What's this?" Arthur wondered. During a pause in the laughter and talk, he heard the sound of galloping hooves and rattling armor. "Perhaps we will have some real-life chivalry this year." He leaned forward in **anticipation.**

Soon everyone in the hall was aware of the mysterious noise outside the door. They whispered uneasily to one another as the sound came closer and closer.

---

[4] Chivalry was the code by which knights conducted themselves during the Middle Ages (A.D. 400-1400). According to the rules of chivalry, knights were expected to be brave, religious, generous, and polite. They were also expected to protect the weak.

[5] (gwin´ ə vir)

[6] (ag´ ra vān)

[7] (ga´ wān)

Suddenly a dark figure mounted on a horse burst through the doorway. All the knights and ladies gasped with surprise.

The strange knight was the tallest man they had ever seen, with a thick and powerful body. But the most amazing thing about the stranger wasn't his size. It was his color. He was green from head to toe. His skin was green, as were his clothes.

A handsome green cloak hung about the knight's shoulders. The hood of the cloak was lined with green fur, and images of green birds and insects were sewn into his clothing. His belt and his horse's saddle were both covered with green silk and set with green jewels. The knight's spurs were golden, but his leather stirrups[8] were dyed green.

Even the knight's horse, a large and powerful animal, was green. It snorted and stamped and tossed its emerald mane. Precious green stones decorated the animal's head and flashed in the light.

The Green Knight wore no helmet or armor. He carried no shield or spear. Instead, he held a holly branch[9] in one hand and a huge green and gold battle-ax[10] in the other. He rode straight into the banquet hall and up to the head table. He spoke to no one. All the guests stared at him in shock. King Arthur and his knights had seen many strange sights, but none so odd as this.

"What kind of man is this?" one knight asked another in a whisper.

"Perhaps he's not a man, but a monster," answered the other knight.

"Or a ghost," murmured yet another knight.

Suddenly the Green Knight spoke in a deep, commanding voice.

---

[8] A spur is a little spiked wheel or knob attached to the rider's heel, used to urge a horse forward. A stirrup is a support to hold a rider's foot.

[9] Holly is an evergreen plant that bears red berries. It is often used in Christmas decorations.

[10] A battle-ax is a weapon, usually with a curved blade.

"Where is the ruler here? I want to have a word or two with him."

All the knights fell into silence. They waited out of courtesy for their king to answer.

"It looks like my adventure has arrived," King Arthur whispered to himself. Then he stepped forward. He was eager to extend a courteous welcome to the Green Knight.

"Welcome to my castle," King Arthur said. "My name is Arthur, and I'm the lord of this hall. Step down, sir. Join my guests. Make yourself comfortable."

"I've not come for comfort," said the Green Knight. "I have come to see the wonder of Camelot with my own eyes. I've heard that the knights of the Round Table are the very models of knighthood. People say they are the bravest and most courteous knights in the world."

"I'm glad to hear that we're so well spoken of," said Arthur **modestly.**

"And you, I am told, are the bravest of them all," said the knight.

"The stories you've heard do me too much honor," said Arthur.

The Green Knight waved his holly branch.

"Look here," said the knight. "You can see by this branch that I've come in peace, not war. What's more, I wear no armor. So what do you say we have a little holiday sport, eh?"

"If you're looking for a fight, you've come to the right place," said Arthur eagerly.

"No, no, I'll have none of that," answered the knight. "I can see that your men aren't the heroes they're said to be. They're just a bunch of beardless boys. If I were armored, not one of these children could match me in a real fight."

Arthur stiffened with anger at the knight's words, but he kept his rage to himself.

"What do you want from us, then?" Arthur asked the knight.

"A party game, that's all," said the knight, laughing. "A little holiday fun."

Then the Green Knight looked around at the gathering. "Is any man here bold enough to trade one blow for another?" he asked, waving his battle-ax about. "If so, step right up! I'll hand this ax to him, and he can strike me with it. I won't even put up a fight. All I ask is that we meet again, a year and a day from now. Then I get to return the blow."

The crowd sat and stared silently. They could hardly believe the **absurdity** of the challenge. How could the Green Knight expect to even pick up his weapon a year and a day from now? Surely one blow from his own ax would kill him on this very night.

The warrior sat on his horse, glaring at the tables of people. He twisted his green beard while he waited for someone to rise. When no one moved, he snorted loudly and began to make fun of the whole crowd.

"What?" he shouted. "Is this Arthur's famous **fellowship** of the Round Table? The bravest knights in all the world? Where's the pride, the fierceness, the chivalry? It's just as I suspected. King Arthur's knights are a bunch of frightened puppies, after all."

King Arthur stepped toward the strange knight.

"You're mistaken, sir," he said. "My men aren't frightened, and neither am I. But we don't much care to kill you for no good reason. Perhaps you should leave before you bring harm to yourself."

"Nonsense!" shouted the knight. "I'll have my game first."

"Very well," said Arthur tiredly. "Give me your ax, and let's be done with it."

The Green Knight stepped down from his horse, towering over the king by a head or more. He handed his mighty ax to King Arthur. The Green Knight was now defenseless and unarmed. But even so, he stood calmly, stroking his beard and showing no fear.

King Arthur raised the ax. But before he could bring

it down on the Green Knight's neck, Sir Gawain stood and spoke out.

"I beg you not to do this, my lord," Gawain said to King Arthur. "Give the ax to me. Let me strike the blow."

"What does it matter which of us does this deed?" answered Arthur impatiently. "Let me do it—and the quicker the better."

"It might be dangerous, my lord," explained Gawain. "This weird fellow might be up to some sort of trick. It's better for me to take the risk than you. You're my king, and I'm only your knight—and a rather poor knight at that."

The king and all knights and ladies in the hall knew that Gawain was only being modest. He was, in fact, the most noble and powerful warrior of the Round Table.

"Take up my challenge if you want," the Green Knight told Gawain. "But you must make a promise. A year and a day from now, you must meet me again and allow me to strike the second blow."

"I will, sir," said Gawain. "That is, if you're still alive. "

King Arthur **reluctantly** agreed to let Gawain take up the challenge. Gawain stepped forward and took the ax. The Green Knight knelt down. He leaned his head forward and lifted his hair so that the back of his green neck was bare. Gawain lifted the ax and held it high. He planted his left foot forward on the ground. Then he let the sharp blade fall quickly on the bare neck.

The blade cut through the green skin, shattered the bones, and cut off the strange knight's head. The head fell to the floor and rolled around under the feet of the nearest warriors. Blood spouted from the headless body—red droplets shining against the green skin and clothing.

Then King Arthur's guests watched in amazement as the Green Knight's body leapt to its feet. The body rushed among the warriors and picked up its head. Then holding his own head in his arms, the Green Knight returned to his horse and mounted. The body was still bleeding from the neck, but the Green Knight behaved as though nothing was wrong.

Wheeling the horse about, the Green Knight waved his head in the air. Then the head opened its eyes. It looked around the crowd and spoke.

"Remember your promise, Sir Gawain," the gruesome head shouted. "A year and a day from now, we must meet again. Then you will let me strike the next blow. You will find me at the Green Chapel on New Year's morning. Meet me there or be known forever as a coward."

Still carrying his head in his hand, the Green Knight turned his horse toward the entryway. Sparks flew from the horse's hooves as it galloped out of the castle.

Everyone at the table began to whisper with alarm. King Arthur, too, was deeply disturbed by what had happened. Even so, he was careful not to show it. He rose from his chair and spoke to all the knights and ladies.

"We've just seen a wonderful **conjurer**'s trick, ladies and gentlemen," he said. "This stranger's little joke was the perfect entertainment for the holidays. Now let us return to our feast."

As if to forget the terrible events they had just witnessed, everyone began chattering again. They passed around the silver dishes of food, and many took double helpings. They spoke of lighthearted matters, as if the Green Knight had never appeared.

But during the festivities, King Arthur's eyes met Gawain's. He could see that Gawain was worried. What had just happened was neither a joke nor a trick. The Green Knight's magic was very real and very dangerous.

"I shouldn't have let Gawain take up that rascal's challenge," King Arthur whispered to Guinevere.

That year passed as most others do. Winter thawed, spring blossomed, and the warm summer provided Camelot with a rich autumn harvest. Then the cold winter winds once again whispered across the land.

The people began to prepare for the Christmas festival. But for Sir Gawain, the hints of the season brought little cheer. They only reminded him of the journey he'd promised to make.

At the beginning of November, Gawain approached King Arthur and all the other knights at the Round Table.

"With your permission, my lord," Gawain said, kneeling, "I'll leave tomorrow to find the man in green.[11] You know the reason for this journey. I made a promise, and a knight always keeps his promise."

King Arthur and his knights talked the matter over seriously. Their hearts were heavy at the idea of Gawain facing the mysterious knight again. Still, Gawain was correct. A knight always kept his promise. The knights sadly agreed that Gawain must make his journey. Only Gawain was able to remain cheerful.

"Come, gentlemen," he said to the rest of the knights. "I'm sure the rest of you would do just as I'm doing. What can any man do but meet his **fate,** whether it prove pleasant or hard?"

"But must you leave so soon?" asked Arthur. "New Year's Day is still two months away."

"No, now's the time for me to go," explained Gawain. "I don't know where this Green Chapel stands, and neither does anyone else here in Camelot. It could take me two months just to find it. I beg you, sir. Let me leave tomorrow."

King Arthur granted Gawain permission. The following morning, Gawain arose and asked for his arms. Over his silk shirt and fur-lined hood, Gawain put on his knightly armor. He began with his steel shoes and knee-pieces. Then he put on chain mail[12] and solid armor to protect his arms and legs. Last he put on a helmet studded[13] with diamonds and other jewels.

---

[11]It was customary for a knight to ask permission to leave his king's castle.
[12]Chain mail is a protective garment made of overlapping metal rings sewn onto leather.

All these steel pieces were highly polished and decorated with gold. Gawain's spurs were gold, and he wore a silk sash[14] around his waist. He picked up his bright red shield and mounted his horse, Gringolet.[15] Gringolet was dressed up too. He wore a saddle and a caparison decorated with gold and silken embroidery.[16]

The people gathered around to say their farewells as Gawain rode Gringolet toward the castle gate. Gawain waved to them cheerfully.

"Pray for my safe return!" he shouted.

Everyone loudly promised to do just that. Then Gringolet's hooves struck fire from the stones as the horse and knight galloped away from Camelot.

The people murmured sadly to one another as their hero rode away.

"What a terrible thing!" said one.

"Whoever heard of a king sending a knight to his death over a holiday joke?" said another.

"Perhaps everything will turn out for the best," said another. "Perhaps the Green Knight has disappeared forever, never to be seen again."

But in their hearts, the people knew that Gawain would find the Green Knight. And they also knew he would keep his part of the bargain. He would let the Green Knight deliver a blow without a fight.

As for Gawain himself, he had no idea where to begin his search. Where might this Green Chapel be? Following his **instincts,** Gawain spurred Gringolet northward. Gawain sped on through the northern countryside. He asked all the people he met whether they had heard of the Green Knight or the Green Chapel. No one had.

As days passed, Gawain journeyed through strange

[13]Studded means decorated or set with jewels or other objects.
[14]A sash is a cloth band worn around the waist or over the shoulder. Sometimes a sash is used to symbolize membership in an organization or military order.
[15](grin gō lā´)
[16]A caparison is an ornamental covering for a horse. Embroidery is a decorative design created by needlework.

lands where no people lived. He was all alone, with no one to keep him company. He traveled over many paths, mountains, cliffs, streams, and rivers. He had to fight wolves, bears, bulls, and boars.[17] He even met and slew his share of dragons and giants. If he were not so brave and powerful, he would surely have been killed.

But the weather was worse than the fighting. Snow and sleet fell upon the knight and his horse. Gawain had to sleep in his armor, often on bare rocks.

The weeks passed by, and Christmas approached. Gawain began to fear that he would not be able to carry out the proper ceremonies and prayers for the holidays. He also began to doubt that he would ever find the Green Knight. As he rode along, he whispered prayers for guidance.

On the morning of Christmas Eve, Gawain rode into a thick, wild forest. He found himself surrounded by huge old oak trees. In the branches, a few silent birds shuddered miserably in the cold. With head hanging in despair, Gawain spurred Gringolet deeper into the dark wilderness.

Then unexpectedly, the knight found himself facing a magnificent castle surrounded by a great moat.[18] Gawain urged Gringolet toward the castle's main gate. The drawbridge was raised and the gates were shut tight. Gawain stopped his horse at the edge of the moat and admired the castle. It was the most beautiful fortress he had ever seen outside of Camelot. But Gawain had yet to see a living soul.

"Hello, there!" Gawain called out. "Is anybody home?"

Suddenly a servant appeared on top of the wall.

"Greetings, stranger," the servant replied pleasantly. "What's your business?"

"Good man, please take a message to the lord of this

---

[17]A boar is a large and often dangerous wild pig.
[18]A moat is a ditch dug around a castle to keep out enemies. It is usually filled with water.

castle," said Gawain. "Tell him that I beg him for a warm place to celebrate the holidays."

"You won't have to beg too hard," said the servant. "My master's plenty generous. I'm sure he'll let you stay here as long as you want."

Then the servant lowered the drawbridge and opened the gates. He and countless other maids and servants came out and knelt down to greet Gawain. Grateful for the warmth of their welcome, Gawain told them to rise. He rode across the bridge into the castle courtyard.

Two servants held Gawain's horse while he dismounted. Meanwhile knights and squires[19] arrived in great numbers and greeted the traveler. Some carried Gawain's helmet, sword, and shield. Others showed him the way to the great hall, where a mighty fire roared in a huge stone fireplace.

In a few moments, the lord of the castle entered. He was a grand, strong man with a thick, brown beard and a broad, **hearty** smile. His battle-worn face was that of a warrior, but his kind voice was that of a gentleman. He greeted Gawain as warmly as his servants, knights, and squires had.

"Welcome, welcome, my brave knight!" said the lord. "I can see that you have traveled long and hard. I want to hear your story, but only when you're rested enough to tell it. You must make yourself comfortable now and consider yourself at home. My castle and everything in it is yours. Use it as you will."

The castle lord led Gawain to a bedroom and left him in the care of servants. The bed was huge, surrounded by silk curtains. The sheets and blankets were embroidered with gold. Colorful tapestries[20] hung on the walls and covered the floor. A fire crackled in the fireplace.

The servants helped Gawain out of his armor. They brought water for his bath and laid out fine clothes for him to wear. After Gawain was dressed, the servants

---

[19]A squire is a knight's helper and attendant.
[20]Tapestries are ornamental fabrics used as wall decorations or carpets.

helped him to a comfortable chair by the fireside. Then they brought him rich food and strong red wine. It was a wonderful feast.

Gawain soon laughed aloud, for the wine went quickly to his head. This was hardly surprising because he was tired from traveling so long. Every bone and muscle in his body ached, and his skin still tingled from the cold.

After dinner, bells were rung in the castle's chapel, announcing the Christmas Eve service. The bells came as a welcome sound to Gawain. Just that morning he had feared that he would have no place to worship on Christmas Eve. Now his prayers had been answered.

Gawain went to the chapel, where the lord of the castle greeted him again. The two of them exchanged gentlemanly **compliments** and sat together for the service.

As Gawain prayed with the castle lord, he noticed two women slip quietly into the chapel. Gawain barely glimpsed the two before they disappeared into a private booth. The women remained there during the rest of the service. When the prayers ended, they slipped out again.

Gawain asked the lord of the castle about the ladies.

"Ah, but I've been terribly rude!" the fine gentleman exclaimed. "I must introduce you to my wife, the lady of the castle."

The castle lord led Gawain to the main hall, where the two ladies and their servants were waiting. The lord's wife wore beautiful scarves and a gorgeous pearl at her throat. Gawain reluctantly thought that she was almost as beautiful as Guinevere.

The older of the two women kept her distance. She didn't say a word to Gawain. She was dressed in black, and her face was almost hidden. But Gawain could see that her skin was ghostly white and wrinkled with age. Her dark eyes were sunken into her face.

The castle lord introduced Gawain to the younger of the two women.

"Sir, meet my wife, the lady of my castle," said the host.

"And whom may I have the honor of meeting?" the

lady questioned politely. "I do hope he is noble and courteous."

"The lowly Sir Gawain of King Arthur's court, at your service," replied Gawain as he gently kissed the lady's hand. "Know that your wish is my command."

"*The* Sir Gawain?" replied the lady with surprise. "My, we are certainly honored! Now we can learn firsthand how to lead the life of chivalry. For we have the **embodiment** of courtly love and nobility in our castle."

The lord, his lady, and Gawain gathered around the fire. More food was brought, and trumpets, drums, and pipes played merrily. The lovely young lady and Gawain were seated side by side. They talked and laughed together and found great pleasure in one another's company. Finally the members of the party bid each other good night and went to bed.

For three days Gawain rested and took part in the Christmas festivities. But when some of the castle lord's guests began to leave, Gawain thought he should go too. He went to the lord to beg his leave.

"As much as I would love to remain through the New Year, I must ask your permission to leave," said Gawain. "I have a certain business to take care of."

"Perhaps I can help," replied the lord with a smile. "What is this business that has you away from home during the time of cheer?"

"I have promised to meet one Green Knight on New Year's Day," said Gawain. "This knight says he can be found at a Green Chapel."

"But I've heard of this Green Knight!" exclaimed the castle lord. "And I know where his Green Chapel is!"

"You do?" asked Gawain with surprise.

"Of course!" said the lord. "He's very famous in these parts."

"Then tell me where I can find his chapel," said Gawain. "I must start on my way there at once."

"Oh, there's no need to rush," said the lord. "Why, the place is not more than two miles away. Stay here until

New Year's Day. You'll have no trouble getting there in time. When the day comes, I'll have one of my servants show you the way."

Gawain was delighted that he could stay longer in this pleasant castle and still keep his promise to the Green Knight.

"Tomorrow morning my guests and I are going out on a hunt," continued the castle lord. "I'd ask you to join us, but you're still tired from your long journey. So stay here. Rest by the fire and take your meals with my wife. I'm sure you'll enjoy the time together."

"Thank you, good sir," said Gawain.

Then the castle lord raised his wine glass.

"Let's make a little agreement," said the lord. "Whatever I catch during the hunt, I'll give to you. And whatever good thing comes your way here in the castle, you'll share with me."

Gawain was always ready to play such castle games. So he agreed. "As long as I am your guest, I will play by your rules," said Gawain. He raised his glass to seal the bargain.

Before dawn the castle lord and all his guests prepared for the hunt. They rounded up their dogs, mounted their horses, and rode off into the forest. But Gawain didn't get up. He was, indeed, still tired from his journey. He lay in bed until the sun came up. Even then, he almost fell asleep again.

But just as he drifted into slumber, Gawain heard a noise at his bedroom door. He peeked out from behind the bed curtains to see who was there. He saw the beautiful lady of the castle come into the room, close the door behind her, and tiptoe toward the bed. She was dressed in her nightgown. Surprised and embarrassed, Gawain pretended to be asleep.

He felt the lady sit down on the edge of the bed. He knew that she was watching him—waiting for him to wake up. He didn't know what to do.

"I can't pretend to be asleep forever," he thought to

himself. "It's best for me to ask her what she's doing here."

So Gawain moved about, opened his eyes, and acted as if he were surprised to see her. The lady smiled at him.

"Good morning, Sir Gawain," she said, laughing. "What a sound sleeper you are! I thought a knight would be more on his guard. If I were an enemy, I could have killed you just now."

"You've nearly killed me with surprise," replied Gawain. "What do you want from me?" he asked as politely as he could.

"To take you prisoner," said the lady jokingly. "Unless you want to put up a fight."

"It's not a knight's way to fight with a lady," Gawain said lightheartedly.

"Oh, so you won't put up a struggle, then?" said the lady, laughing again. "Very well. I'll tie you to the bed here and now. Then let's see you try to escape."

"There's no need for that," said Gawain. "Since I refuse to fight you, I'm your prisoner already."

"So you are," said the lady.

Gawain was puzzled and disturbed. The lady was beautiful and Gawain certainly enjoyed her company. Even so, he was the castle lord's guest and did not dare give in to the lady's charms. But Gawain wondered if he could resist if she tempted him.

"You've taken me by surprise, fair lady," he said. "Perhaps you'd be willing to leave me for a moment and let me arise and get dressed. I'd feel more comfortable talking to you then."

The lady laughed some more. "And give up my control over you?" she said. "Oh no, not for a moment. I've heard so much about you, Sir Gawain. I've heard stories of your honor and your courage.

"And now you're here and we're alone," she continued, bending closer to him. "My lord and his men are far away. The servants are in their beds. The door is fastened with a strong bolt. Didn't my lord command you to make everything in his castle your own?"

Indeed, Gawain was extremely tempted by the lady. Even so, he drew away from her.

"Good lady, the stories you've heard about me do me too much honor," he said. "The truth is, I'm a poor excuse for a knight and unworthy of your favors. It is I who should be serving you—and I can do that best with conversation."

So the knight and the lady sat and talked. They spoke of many things until the morning was half over. Gawain found the lady's conversation charming and pleasant.

At last the lady rose to leave. She turned to Gawain with a **mischievous** smile.

"I don't believe you're really the great Sir Gawain," she said.

"Why not?" asked the knight.

"Gawain is said to be courteous. He'd ask a lady for some keepsake to remember her by. A kiss, perhaps."

Gawain thought about the matter for a moment. He didn't wish to seem impolite, and a kiss seemed innocent enough.

"Very well," said Gawain. "I'll kiss you under orders. It would not be knightly of me to disobey."

And so the lady came back from the doorway toward the bed. She bent down and kissed Gawain. Then she left the bedroom.

That night the lord of the castle returned from the hunt. He and his guests gathered in the great hall and showed Gawain the deer they had killed.

"A successful hunt, eh, Sir Gawain?" boasted the lord. "And as we agreed, this excellent kill is yours."

Gawain thanked the lord and then fell silent. He didn't know what to say. Gawain felt it was his duty to tell the lord about what had happened between him and the lady—to tell the lord his wife had tempted him. But Gawain didn't wish to insult either the lord or his lady. So he quickly thought of another way of telling what had happened.

"I must keep my part of the bargain," Gawain said to the lord. "I promised to share whatever good thing came my way today in the castle—and here it is."

Gawain clasped the lord's neck and kissed him. The lord looked surprised.

"Where did you get this prize?" asked the lord.

"I can't tell you," said Gawain as he shook his head.

"Why not?"

"That wasn't part of our agreement."

The lord studied Gawain's expression for a moment. Then the lord's face broke into a slow smile. At last he began to laugh.

"I did the right thing," thought Gawain. "My host now understands what happened, and he's grateful for my honesty and **discretion.** I haven't lied to him, but I haven't embarrassed him either."

Gawain followed the lord to dinner. Later that night, they drank wine and made the same agreement for the next day.

The following morning the lord and his guests left for the hunt again. And the lord's lady came to Gawain's bedroom and tempted him, just as she had the morning before. And as before, Gawain and the lady talked the morning away. But unlike the first morning, the lady kissed Gawain twice before leaving.

That night the lord of the castle brought Gawain a boar he had killed in the hunt. And Gawain filled his part of the bargain by giving the lord two kisses. The lord smiled and laughed again. As before, he seemed to be grateful for Gawain's quiet honesty.

The next morning the lord was gone to hunt before dawn. And again, the lady came to Gawain's room. He was more tempted by her than ever. In fact, he had fallen quite in love with her.

"Lady, this will be the last chance we have to talk together," Gawain told her. "Tomorrow is New Year's Day—the day I must leave your kind company."

The lady looked at Gawain worriedly.

"Then you must leave me a gift," the lady said. "Courtesy demands it."

"But I have no gift with me," replied Gawain. "I didn't come prepared for giving gifts to fine ladies."

"Then you must take a gift from me," she said. And she offered him a beautiful golden ring set with a gleaming jewel. But Gawain refused the ring. Then she removed her green silk belt and held it out to Gawain.

"Take this, then," she said. "Take it as a token of my love."

Gawain shook his head. "That would be wrong of me, my lady," he said.

"But you don't understand," the lady insisted. "This belt has magical powers. The wearer of this belt can't be harmed. No matter how deadly the blow from sword or blade, your body would suffer no injury."

Gawain thought the matter over carefully. The truth was, he was deeply frightened about facing the Green Knight. He had promised to let the Green Knight strike him without a fight. Surely Gawain would die from such a stroke. Was there any harm in accepting this token—particularly if it was magical?

"Thank you, lady," Gawain said. "I accept your gift."

"But tell no one I have done this," said the lady. "This must remain our secret. Do you promise not to tell?"

"I promise," said Gawain.

With a smile, the lady kissed Gawain three times and left the room.

That night the lord returned. But before the lord could present his kill, Gawain gave the lord three kisses.

"Well done," was the lord's reply. "But I am afraid that all I have to offer you tonight is this sorry fox pelt.[21] And I was lucky to catch this sly fellow—he about got away from me."

"But no matter," continued the lord as he slapped Gawain on the back. "Let's celebrate your last night with us."

The lord's easy manner made Gawain uneasy. "Does

---

[21] A pelt is the skin of an animal.

he know of the lady's other gift—the magical belt?" he wondered. But Gawain soon forgot the matter. He had his meeting with the Green Knight to worry about.

That night brought a great feast in celebration of New Year's Eve. Gawain announced his leaving to the lord and all his guests. And he thanked everybody for their kindness, generosity, and friendship.

As he had promised, the lord assigned a servant to show Gawain the way to the Green Chapel. Everyone expressed sadness that Gawain was leaving—everyone except the old woman with the ghostly white face and black eyes. As always, she stood apart from the others and remained silent.

When Gawain awoke the next morning, he could hear a great storm raging outside. He lay in bed and listened for awhile, but finally he got up and dressed. He sent his servant to saddle and ready the horses. He put on his armor, which had been cleaned and polished during his stay. He also put the lady's green silk belt around his waist.

At the castle gate, the servant held Gringolet waiting. The horse was now well fed and rested. Gawain mounted Gringolet and took up his shield. The gates were opened, the drawbridge lowered, and the two lonely horsemen rode out of the castle. The storm let up somewhat, but a steady drizzle kept falling.

Gawain and the servant passed by high banks and bare trees. They climbed cliffs and made their way through thick mists. They followed a lonely road to the top of a high hill covered with snow. Then the servant asked the knight to halt.

"We're not far from the place you seek," the servant said.

"Why have we stopped, then?" asked Gawain urgently. "I have a promise to keep."

"I know this Green Knight. He is an awful brute—dangerous and powerful. He would as soon lop off your head as look at you. No one can defeat the Green Knight.

You will surely die if you meet him."

"What are you trying to tell me?" asked Gawain.

"I've grown to admire and like you, sir," said the servant. "So has everybody else in the castle. Don't go to the Green Chapel. Go home or run some other way. I'll keep your secret to the grave."

Gawain clasped the servant's hand.

"Thank you for your concern, my friend," said Gawain. "And may you have good fortune for wishing me safety. But I am a knight. Even if you kept my secret, how could I live with myself if I ran away? No, I must meet the Green Knight. I promised."

Gawain put on his helmet and picked up his spear. He said good-bye to the servant and rode where the man had directed him to go. Gawain and Gringolet followed a path through huge rocks to the bottom of a wild and rough valley. The clouds overhead seemed to rest upon the overhanging cliffs.

Gawain saw no place to rest, much less any sign of the Green Chapel. Then he noticed a small mound on the bank near a stream. He guided Gringolet to the mound, dismounted, and tied the horse to a tree branch. Then Gawain walked around the mound, wondering what it was.

Gawain saw that there were several openings in the mound, and that they led deep into the ground. He could see no end to the tunnels as they wound their way into the darkness.

"Can this be the Green Chapel?" wondered Gawain. "It looks like no holy place I've ever seen. In fact, it looks more like some place where the devil himself might live."

Then Gawain heard a loud, awful noise from the hill beyond the brook. It sounded like someone sharpening a huge blade against a grindstone.[22] The terrible noise rumbled and rang throughout the valley. The noise made Gawain shiver with fear, but he shouted out bravely.

"Who's up there?" Gawain called. "Come out and

---

[22] A grindstone is a flat circular piece of sandstone used to shape or sharpen objects, such as blades.

show yourself. My name is Gawain, and I've come from King Arthur's mighty fellowship. If you've got any business with me, let's get it done now or never."

"Wait," answered a booming voice from the cliff above Gawain's head. "I'll be ready for you in a moment."

The grating noise continued for another few seconds. Then a man appeared, seeming to step right out of the mountain itself. It was the huge knight with skin and clothing all of green. He held a freshly sharpened ax, with a blade at least four feet wide. The blade was bound to the ax's wooden handle with strong leather straps.

The Green Knight strode through the snow toward Gawain. When he arrived at the stream, he did not wade through. He put the head of the ax on the ground and vaulted over the swiftly flowing water.

"Welcome, good man," the Green Knight said. "I see you can be trusted to keep an agreement. I'm sure you remember your promise. Last year I let you strike me with a blow. Now you must let me strike you in return. Take off your helmet and don't give me any more arguments than I gave you."

"I'll make no complaint," said Gawain. "Get ready to strike. I'll stand still and let you do as you will."

Gawain bowed and bared the back of his neck. He was determined not to tremble from fear. The Green Knight lifted his grim weapon high, ready to strike with all the power in his body. He swung the blade downward. But Gawain caught a glimpse of the blade as it swished near. He **flinched** slightly and moved his shoulders. The Green Knight let the blow swerve aside, missing Gawain's neck.

"You are not Sir Gawain," the Green Knight said **mockingly.** "Gawain would never shy away from danger. Why, you shrink with fear before you even feel any pain. Gawain would never show such cowardice. And I didn't shrink or flee when Gawain swung his ax at me."

"Let me remind you of something," Gawain said.

"When my head drops down on the stones, I won't be able to pick it up and ride away with it. But never mind that. I flinched once, but I won't do it again. So let's get on with it. I won't make another move until your ax has struck me."

Looking fierce and grim, the Green Knight raised the ax high. He swung a mighty blow, but he didn't cut Gawain. Instead, he stopped the swing before the weapon could strike. This time, Gawain stood as still as a stone. He didn't flinch at all.

"I see you've gotten back your nerve," said the Green Knight, laughing harshly.

"Why didn't you do it, then?" Gawain asked angrily. "I don't believe you can bring yourself to go through with it. I believe you've lost your nerve."

"You speak boldly," said the Green Knight. "And bold words deserve a bold answer. Here comes your answer!"

And the Green Knight swung a mighty blow. But he didn't cut off Gawain's head. The sharp blade only nicked Gawain's neck. It cut through the skin and into the muscle without touching bone.

Gawain saw his own red blood dripping in the snow. It took him just a moment to realize he was still alive. Then he leapt to his feet and swiftly moved away from the Green Knight. He put on his helmet and picked up his shield and sword.

"Don't you dare strike me again!" Gawain yelled. "I took your ax stroke without fighting back. That takes care of my part of the agreement. If you strike now, you'd better be ready for a good, hard fight."

The Green Knight moved back. He put his ax handle on the ground and leaned on it calmly.

"Don't be angry with me, fellow warrior," the Green Knight said. "You're quite right. You've kept your part of the bargain. I won't strike again. Fair's fair."

Gawain felt dizzy from confusion and surprise.

"Who are you?" he cried out to the Green Knight.

"Why have you tested me this way?"

The Green Knight smiled.

"Do you mean you haven't figured it out by now?" the Green Knight asked.

Then Gawain realized the truth.

"You're the lord of the castle, aren't you?" said Gawain.

The Green Knight nodded and smiled more broadly.

"That's right, my friend," the Green Knight said. "Remember the agreement we made back at my castle? The first night, you kept your word. You gave me the kiss you received from my wife. And so my first blow was not intended to harm you. On the second night, you gave me the two kisses my wife gave you. And so my second blow did you no harm. You see, I sent her to tempt you, to test your **virtue.**

"But, Gawain, you failed me on the third night. That belt you are wearing belonged to my wife. She made it with her own hands. I know it well. She gave it to you, but you only gave me her three kisses. You kept the belt for yourself—not out of **lust,** but out of fear. You hoped it would save your life. And because of that failure, I cut you on my third blow."

Gawain was furious with himself. He untied the belt and slung it toward the Green Knight.

"My fear of death made me lie and play you false,"[23] Gawain said. "Please forgive me. I curse myself for the coward I am."

The Green Knight threw back his head and laughed.

"Come now," said the Green Knight heartily. "Don't be so hard on yourself. It was only a small failure, so I only gave you a small wound. You can be sure of this, my friend. If you had wronged me seriously, you would not be alive right now. You've received your punishment at the edge of my weapon. I think that makes us even."

"How can you change forms so?" asked Gawain with amazement. "Where do you get your power?"

[23]To *play false* means to betray or deceive someone.

"Do you remember seeing my wife in the company of an elderly woman?" replied the Green Knight.

"Yes," said Gawain.

"The woman's name is Morgan le Fay, and she is an amazing magician—a student of the mighty Merlin himself.[24] This whole game between you and me was her idea. She sent me to Camelot to test the pride and virtue of the Round Table. I'll tell her how well you did. She'll be impressed."

Then the Green Knight held out the belt.

"Here, my friend," the Green Knight said. "Take this belt as a gift from me. It is green, like I am. It will remind you of me and what happened here. Take it as a token of the adventure of the Green Chapel."

"I will take it as a reminder of my failures," Gawain said as he took the belt. "Every time I see it, I will remember how fear caused me to be unfaithful to you."

"You are welcome to return to the castle with me," said the Green Knight. "We'll finish celebrating the New Year. And you can chat with my wife again, now that you know what part she had in this little play of ours."

"No, I must return to Camelot," said Gawain. "But thank you for your **hospitality.** And please give my greetings to your noble lady. She's taught me a valuable lesson—that a knight can always be tricked by a woman's cleverness."

Gawain mounted Gringolet and took his leave of the Green Knight. On his way back to Camelot, he had many wonderful adventures. But none could compare to his strange stay at the lord's palace and his final meeting with the Green Knight.

When Gawain entered Arthur's banquet hall, all the knights rose from their seats. They rushed to greet him. Arthur wept tears of joy, for he had feared that his most noble knight had been killed. Everybody began asking

---

[24](mōr´ gan le fā) Morgan le Fay and Merlin commonly appear in legends about Arthur. Merlin was King Arthur's protector and teacher. Morgan le Fay is sometimes portrayed as Arthur's sister or half sister. She is usually seen as Arthur's enemy.

him questions all at once. Gawain laughed.

"Sit down, gentlemen," he said. "I've got quite a story to tell."

It is said that poor Gawain wept when he told the knights of the Round Table about failing his test. Then he told them that he would wear the green belt the rest of his life. This would remind him of his weakness.

But to Gawain's surprise, all the knights of the Round Table began to wear green belts as well. They didn't want Sir Gawain to feel alone in his humility. After all, he was still their model of nobility and chivalry.

INSIGHTS

The origin of "Sir Gawain and the Green Knight" is a bit of a mystery. The story was found in a single manuscript along with three other poems. The name of the author wasn't recorded. So because one of the other poems was called "The Pearl," the author was named the Pearl Poet.

Though the author's name and position are unknown, scholars have made some guesses about this person. He was probably a male who lived in the mid-14th century. And judging by the language of the poem, it seems likely he came from northwest England. Scholars also guess that he was well-read and familiar with the courtly life of the English nobility.

Some scholars also believe that the Pearl Poet's work may have been largely unknown during his lifetime. The nameless poet would be pleased that many critics today rank his poems among the finest in the literature of the Middle Ages (A.D. 400-1400).

"Sir Gawain and the Green Knight" is a romance. At first this term was used to describe any long story in French verse.

By the end of the Middle Ages in the 15th century, that meaning had changed. Romance then referred to a fantastic story set in a distant time or place. Such a story usually involved brave knights, fair maidens, and awful monsters. It is in this sense that "Sir Gawain and the Green Knight" is a romance.

During the Middle Ages, only a man born to a noble family could become a knight. But birth wasn't the only qualification. In fact, the road to knighthood was long and slow.

First, the young man became a page and learned proper behavior with ladies. Next the knight-to-be became a squire. At this stage he mastered the skills of war. When the squire reached the age of twenty or so, it was time for him to be knighted in an elaborate ceremony.

The young knight vowed to follow the high standards of chivalry. According to the code of chivalry, a knight was expected to be courageous at all times. He was also supposed to be loyal to his king, relatives, friends, and the lady he loved.

Above all, a knight was expected to be a man of honor. He should win and deserve the respect of other nobles.

Perhaps the tales of the Round Table were so popular because they celebrated the code of chivalry. Knights in real life rarely met the standards of Arthur's men. Yet it was flattering to be put in the same category as those legendary heroes.

While many of King Arthur's knights did set high standards, they weren't without flaws. Yet their very failures made them more interesting. In this myth, Gawain passes part of his test but fails another. This failure makes him more sympathetic—and a better person in the end.

Other heroic Arthurian characters had their flaws too. Lancelot—one of Arthur's strongest knights—fell in love with Queen Guinevere.

Even King Arthur himself made a terrible mistake— probably the most terrible in all of Camelot. When Arthur was a young man, he fell in love with an evil woman. This woman, Morgan le Fay, was not only already married but she was a witch as well. And though Arthur didn't know it, she was also his half sister.

As a result of their union, Mordred was born to Morgan le Fay. When Mordred grew to manhood, he

continued

succeeded in turning the knights of Arthur's fellowship against each other. You can read the story of Mordred's treachery in the final selection of this volume, "The Death of King Arthur."

THOR THE BRIDE

VOCABULARY PREVIEW

Below is a list of words that appear in the story. Read the list and get to know the words before you read the story.

adamant—stubborn; firm
analyze—examine; break something down into parts
cordially—politely; kindly
craggy—uneven; rough
demurred—objected; protested
eligible—qualified; available
finicky—choosy; fussy
gusto—energy; vitality
indignation—anger; outrage
knack—talent; gift
lusty—forceful; passionate
mere—simple
physique—structure of the body; figure
resplendent—dazzling; glorious
rogue—rascal; imp
sagely—wisely; with good judgment
sarcastically—mockingly; insultingly
substantial—stout; solid
technically—legally; according to set standards
uncouth—rude; vulgar

Main Characters

Freya—goddess of love
Heimdall—a wise god
Logi—a giant
Loki—trickster god
Thor—god of thunder; protector of human race
Thrym—a giant

The Scene

The story begins in Asgard, the Norse land of the gods. Then the action moves to Jotunheim, the land of the giants.

THOR
the Bride

The Norse gods can't get along without Thor's hammer. It is one of the few weapons that protects them from the giants. So when Thor's hammer turns up missing—well the gods will do almost anything to get it back. But will Thor, the mighty god of thunder, go along with their unusual scheme?

Where's my hammer?"

The loud, lusty, red-headed god Thor roared his displeasure. His shouting echoed throughout Asgard,[1] the dwelling place of the gods. Thor searched Asgard's many halls and mansions. He asked all the gods he met if they knew where his hammer was. But no one had seen it.

Now this hammer was no ordinary carpenter's tool. Thor was Odin's[2] son and the god of thunder. The hammer—which he called Mjollnir[3]—was his weapon, and he much preferred it to a sword or spear. Along with his lightning bolts, the magic hammer was Thor's most prized possession.

Thor used his hammer to battle evil demons. Once he

[1] (as´ gard)
[2] (ō´ din) Odin is the chief Scandinavian god.
[3] (myōl´ ner)

used it to kill a giant who tried to steal the sun, the moon, and the goddess Freya.[4] He also used it in his role as protector of the human race. In thanks, humankind named a day of the week after him—Thursday.

Thor realized that he wouldn't find his hammer in Asgard. So he gave up his search and went to find Loki.

Now Loki was a tricky god, and he was often in trouble. When things went wrong in Asgard, the gods usually blamed him. If Loki wasn't actually behind the mischief, he at least would have some idea who was.

"Look here, you little **rogue**," Thor roared when he found Loki. "Someone's taken my hammer, and I want it back!"

"Surely you don't think I stole it," replied Loki with a little twinkle in his eye.

"Not for a minute," said Thor. "You're too smart to get on my bad side. But somebody did steal it, and I want to know who!"

"Stole your hammer!" murmured Loki, shaking his head. "Oh dear, oh dear! What's this universe coming to when the gods themselves aren't safe from theft?"

"Save me the speeches," snarled Thor. "You're no friend of mine, nor of anybody else I know. But you're smart, and you like a challenge. And I know you can cook up some way to help me."

"Perhaps, perhaps," said Loki, scratching his chin. "Let's examine the possibilities, shall we? Your hammer is nowhere in Asgard, so it must be somewhere else in the universe."

"Oh, indeed!" exclaimed Thor **sarcastically.** "Well, that does narrow it down, doesn't it?"

"Patience, patience," said Loki. "We can be pretty sure that no human could have taken it. Why, none of them could so much as pick the thing up. That narrows our possibilities to one. Your thief must have been a giant."[5]

---

[4] Freya is the Scandinavian goddess of love.
[5] The giants were a race of supernatural beings who appeared on earth before the gods.

"A giant!" exclaimed Thor, raising an eyebrow.

"Well, it makes sense, doesn't it?" said Loki. "The giants have always been the enemies of the gods. And they have a **knack** for stealing things."

"But how are we to get my hammer back?" asked Thor.

"I've got an idea," said Loki. "First, I must have a chat with Freya."

Freya, the love goddess, was one of the most popular immortals. The day Friday was named after her. Freya loved fine clothing, and she had a splendid cloak that Loki had long been itching to get his hands on. It was made from falcon feathers and had magical powers.

"Someone has stolen Thor's hammer," Loki told Freya.

"Oh, have they?" said Freya playfully. "I hadn't heard." Of course, none of the gods had failed to hear the news. Thor had bellowed it all over Asgard.

"I've got a plan to get it back," said Loki. "But I'll need the use of your cloak."

"You'll bring it back, won't you?" asked Freya with suspicion in her voice. "It seems there's been a lot of theft lately."

Loki rubbed his hands with envy. Indeed, stealing the wonderful cloak had crossed his mind. But he knew he would only get into serious trouble by doing so.

"I swear to you I won't steal it," said Loki through clenched teeth.

"And I believe you," said Freya, taking off the cloak and handing it to Loki. "But remember this. If you break your word, you'll have a lot of angry gods to deal with."

So Loki borrowed Freya's falcon cloak. He put it on and spread his arms so that the feathers caught the wind. Loki rose into the air and flew away from Asgard. The falcon feathers whistled in the wind as Loki rushed high into the air.

Loki flew on and on, all the way to Jotunheim,[6] the

---

[6] (yot´ in hīm or yot´ in hăm) The land of the giants was said to be far to the northwest where the water joins the end of the world.

land of the giants. He found the lord of the giants, Thrym,[7] twisting strands of gold together. Thrym was making a leash to hold his hound. When Thrym looked up and saw Loki, he greeted the god **cordially** enough.

"How is everything at Asgard?" asked Thrym. "How are all your marvelous gods, dwarfs, elves, and such?"

"Things aren't well in Asgard," said Loki, crossing his arms sternly. "And I think you know why."

"I'm sure I don't know what you mean," said Thrym, putting down his golden leash and trimming his horse's mane. "Tell me, what brings you to Jotunheim all alone? It's not often that we giants get social calls from gods."

"I'm looking for a hammer—Thor's hammer," replied Loki. "Some thief has stolen his favorite weapon."

The giant said nothing. He just hummed and kept on grooming his horse.

"It was you, wasn't it?" said Loki, breaking the silence.

Thrym shook his head and grinned widely. "You're too smart for me, Loki," he said. "You found me out. Not that it will do you any good. I've buried Thor's hammer eight miles down in the earth. No man or god will find it."

"Why would you do that?" Loki asked with alarm. "You know how unpleasant the god of storm and rain and thunder can be when he's angry."

"Unpleasant for you, maybe," said Thrym. "I don't have to live with him. And I don't imagine the gods of Asgard will go to war with the giants over a **mere** hammer. The thing is mine now, and I intend to keep it. Unless..." Thrym paused.

"Unless what?"

"Unless Freya agrees to be my wife."

Loki stared at the giant in disbelief. "But that's impossible!" he cried. "Everybody wants to marry Freya. She's constantly turning **eligible** suitors down. She's turned away others of your race before. The giants and gods have even had wars over her. What makes you think

[7] (thrim)

she'll marry you now?"

"Well, she'd better marry me," said Thrym with a sly wink. "Otherwise, Thor will stay very angry."

At a loss for words, Loki wrapped the falcon cloak around his shoulders and lifted his arms. He rose into the air and flew back toward Asgard, feathers whistling all the way. He fretted as he flew. He knew that Freya, the love goddess, was very choosy. She wasn't going to marry some **uncouth** giant.

Freya had once been Odin's wife. But Odin had quickly realized that she was more fond of fine clothes and jewels than she was of him. So Odin had given Freya up for his present queen, Frigga.[8] This made Freya **technically** available for marriage.

"But what chance is there that she'd agree to this match?" wondered Loki as he flew along. "And how shall I deal with Thor if she doesn't agree?"

As Loki approached Asgard, he could see Thor waiting for him atop the walls.

"You'd better bring good news!" Thor roared, rushing up before Loki had properly landed.

"Yes, yes," said Loki, brushing himself off. "Give me a minute to catch my breath."

"No, tell me at once, before you forget something," insisted Thor. "Or before you can think up some clever lie."

"Thrym has your hammer," said Loki.

"Then why didn't you bring it back?" asked Thor.

"I couldn't," explained Loki. "Thrym buried it deep in the ground. No one can possibly find it."

"So what can we do?" moaned Thor miserably.

"First we must talk to Freya," said Loki. "In return for your hammer, Thrym wants Freya for his wife."

"Freya for his wife!" grumbled Thor. "Oh, we'll have a fine time getting her to go along with that!"

"We'll just have to try," said Loki. "I suggest we take the aggressive approach."

[8] (frig´ ga)

"The aggressive approach? What's that?" asked Thor.

"Just come with me, and let me do the talking," said Loki.

So Loki and Thor went to visit Freya.

"Get dressed for a journey, Freya," said Loki, clapping his hands commandingly. "You're coming with us to Jotunheim."

"Jotunheim?" exclaimed Freya. "The land of the giants? Why should we go to that poor excuse for a world?"

"For a wedding," said Loki.

"A wedding!" exclaimed Freya with a smile. "Oh, well, that's different. I do love weddings. Whose is it?"

"Yours," said Loki. "Thrym wants you for his wife. He won't return Thor's hammer unless he gets you in return. So come on. We've got no time to lose. Put on your bridal veil and let's get going."

"A giant?" cried Freya with **indignation.** "You want me to marry a giant? You must be crazy—or think I'm crazy. Do you really think I'm that hard up for a husband?"

Freya stamped her foot so furiously that all the halls of Asgard shook. She let out such a snort of rage that her necklace broke into two pieces. And this was no ordinary necklace. It was a solid gold ring that the dwarfs had made. Thor and Loki fled the goddess' wrath in terror.

"Was that what you call 'the aggressive approach'?" asked Thor as he and Loki retreated into the halls of Asgard.

"She's more **adamant** than I expected," observed Loki.

"Well, she's got a point, you know," said Thor. "A goddess marrying a giant! It just isn't done! Still, I'd do anything to get my hammer back."

"You may have to," grumbled Loki. "I'm running out of ideas. Let's go talk to the other gods."

So Thor asked Odin to call a council of the gods. Thor told everyone about Thrym's demand. Then he asked for their suggestions. There was much discussion of the matter. But it was Heimdall,[9] the wisest god of all, who came up with the best idea.

"Let's **analyze** the situation," Heimdall said. "Thor must have his hammer back. But Thrym will only return it if Freya agrees to be his bride. And Freya, quite naturally, refuses to play her part."

"So what can we do?" asked Thor.

"Trick Thrym," said Heimdall **sagely.** "Make him think he's getting what he wants."

"How?" asked Loki. "By sending another goddess in disguise? We won't have much luck finding volunteers."

"That's not quite what I meant," said Heimdall. "Let's put the bridal veil on Thor himself."

All the gods laughed. Thor was a large and muscular god with a red beard and masses of red hair. There was nothing feminine about him.

"You'd all like that, wouldn't you?" shouted Thor, waving his fist angrily. "You'd get a good laugh from that."

"Well, do you have any better ideas?" asked Heimdall.

Thor didn't. Neither did the other gods. So they quieted down and thought it over. They studied Thor's **physique,** looking for a way to make him appear more feminine.

"We'd have to cover those," said Loki, pointing to Thor's hairy and muscular legs.

"A long skirt will do the trick," said Heimdall.

"We could repair Freya's dwarf-made necklace and have Thor wear it," said Loki. "Everybody knows that it belongs to the goddess of love."

"Good," said Heimdall. "We'll give him a perky little cap, and pin jewelry to his dress. And we'll put rings on his fingers to hide his big knuckles."

"Still, his face will be a problem," mused Loki. "It's a little on the **craggy** side."

[9] (hām´ dal)

"Indeed," said Heimdall. "The beard has got to go."

"The beard!" roared Thor. "Look here, I'll have none of that!"

"Well, you can wear a bridal veil," said Heimdall.

"A very thick bridal veil," added Loki.

"What do you think I am, some kind of fool?" roared Thor. "If I let you dress me up in all these girlish clothes, I'll never hear the last of your laughter."

"Hold your tongue," said Loki sternly. "Giants will be living in Asgard soon if we don't get your hammer back. We won't be able to hold them off without your magic weapon."

So the thunderer quieted down and let the other gods dress him up. They put a long skirt on him and pinned jewels to his dress. They put rings on his big fingers, and they placed Freya's necklace around his neck. Then they put a thick veil over Thor's face.

At last they succeeded in making Thor look as much like the gorgeous Freya as possible. The gods stood back and admired their handiwork. They told Thor what a lovely bride he was. As for Thor, he grumbled and complained in a most unfeminine fashion.

"If it will make you feel any better, I'll dress up too," said Loki reluctantly. "I'll go with you to Jotunheim, disguised as your servant girl."

So the other gods dressed Loki as a woman too. This job was a great deal easier than disguising Thor—Loki being a good deal thinner than Thor.

Finally Thor and Loki were ready to leave. Thor harnessed his goats to his chariot. Then he called out in a dramatic voice, "To Jotunheim, right away!"

The goats dashed across the mountains, making the sound of thunder for which Thor was famous. Thor threw a few lightning bolts to add to the drama.

Meanwhile in Jotunheim, Thrym was decorating the hall, quite sure that Freya would gladly join him. A wedding feast was prepared for the many guests who were invited. When evening came, Thrym's "bride" and her servant girl arrived. Horns[10] of ale were poured for all the giants.

Thrym seated his bride and her servant girl at the banquet table. The giants watched with amazement as the bride-to-be ate her meal. She ate a huge ox—whole. Eight salmon also disappeared behind the bridal veil. Then she ate all the cakes she could get her hands on and guzzled down three vats of ale.

"By the heavens!" cried Thrym, gleefully thumping the table with his fist. "Look at the old girl put the grub away! My, but she's a hearty wench!"

"Freya hasn't eaten for eight days," explained the servant girl nervously. "She's been so eager to marry you that she wouldn't eat."

"Well, she's a fine, tough woman with a lot of **gusto!**" exclaimed Thrym. You see, giants appreciated **lusty** eaters and drinkers. In fact, as part of the wedding festivities, they had planned contests to see who could eat the most.

As it happened, the giants called on the bride's servant girl to compete against a giant named Logi.[11]

"I don't know," Loki **demurred,** "I'm not very good at eating contests."

But the giants called out over and over, "Eat! Eat!" as they hammered the tables with their large fists.

"Okay, Okay," grumbled Loki. "Show me how to play."

The giants put the servant girl on one end of a huge trough filled with food. The giant Logi stood at the other end. Then the two contestants were ordered to eat as fast as they could. The one who ate the most would be the winner.

Loki thought he was doing pretty well as he shoveled food into his mouth. Indeed, the giant and servant girl met at the middle of the trough.

"It must be a tie," thought Loki as he stood up from the trough.

---

[10]Horns are drinking vessels made from hollowed out animal horns.
[11](lō´ gē)

But then Loki frowned. Being a **finicky** eater, he'd picked all the meat from the bones. But the giant had eaten the meat, the bones, and the trough too. Of course, Logi the giant was declared the winner.

"Even though you lost, you're still a pretty good eater," Thrym said to the servant girl after the contest. Then he pulled Loki aside and said in a low voice, "But you know, I don't remember Freya looking like this the last time I saw her. I thought she was more...dainty."

"A...er...what can I say?" said the servant girl. "Freya's been gaining weight just for you. She knew you'd like a more **substantial** wife."

"Well, she's certainly filled out nicely," observed Thrym. "But you know, I'd like just one little kiss before the ceremony."

"I wouldn't try that if I were you," said the servant girl quickly. "Freya is very shy. She might run away."

"All the more reason to steal a little peek at the beauty," said the giant. Thrym reached out to lift the bridal veil. The bride grasped the veil and turned her head away as if from shyness. But Thrym managed to pull the veil aside enough to see her eyes. He jumped back quickly.

"Why are Freya's eyes so fierce?" asked Thrym. "Her eyes blaze at me with fire!"

"Freya hasn't slept for eight days," explained the servant girl. "She's been so eager to be here with you that she couldn't sleep."

At that moment, the giant's sister came into the banquet hall. She walked up to the bride-to-be.

"What lovely rings you're wearing!" said Thrym's sister. "And so many of them too! Give them all to me right now. In return, I'll be your friend."

Thrym's sister reached out to take the rings. The bride drew back, as if from fear. The bride's servant girl froze like a statue. Thrym thought he'd better do something to break the tension.

"Bring Thor's mighty hammer here at once," commanded Thrym. "After all, it was that marvelous object that brought this **resplendent** goddess to our land. We will lay the hammer on the lady's knee. It can rest there as we take our marriage vows."

So the hammer was brought and laid upon the lap of the bride-to-be. Slowly, her hand reached out and took the hammer by the handle. Then the sound of thunder and laughter roared out from beneath the bridal veil. The thunder god cast off the veil and rose up in his full fury.

"I don't think Freya is feeling like getting married just today," said Loki to Thrym. "But it's been fun anyway."

Thor swung one blow and laid the giant Thrym low. He tapped the greedy sister's head with a second blow. Then he let loose his anger upon the rest of the relatives gathered for the celebration.

Then the giants began to gang up on the two gods. So Thor took his magic hammer and dashed toward his chariot. Loki ran after him, desperate to keep up. They both leaped into the chariot, and Thor's goats charged across the mountains. With thunder and lightning and rainstorms following them all the way, Thor and Loki returned to Asgard with the precious hammer.

INSIGHTS

The story of Thor's hammer is part of pre-Christian mythology belonging to the ancient people of Scandinavia—modern-day Norway, Sweden, Denmark, and Finland. These people were known to other Europeans of the time as Vikings or Norsemen (men of the North). From about the middle of the 8th century, bands of Vikings began to roam the waterways in their longboats. They were greatly feared because they raided and plundered much of the known world.

The word *Viking* probably comes from the word *vik,* which means "creek" in Scandinavian languages. The name may have arisen from the raiding habits of the Vikings. They were known to sail their ships into creeks and bays and then sweep out to attack passing boats. Vikings also traveled by creeks to sneak into the country-side and pull off surprise land attacks.

The well-known horned helmets usually pictured on Vikings were probably never worn during battle. They were too heavy and clumsy. Most likely, the helmets were mainly used during religious ceremonies.

One of the most famous Vikings is Leif Ericsson. He and his men landed on the North American continent almost 500 years before Columbus. Later groups of Vikings tried to settle there, but determined Native Americans probably drove them away.

We would know little of the Norse mythology but for two manuscripts discovered in Iceland in the 1600s. These manuscripts are known as the *Poetic Edda* and the *Prose Edda.* They contain some of the few written accounts of the Norse gods.

It is a wonder that these few manuscripts were ever written. It seems that as the Christian religion spread throughout Northern Europe, the pagan (pre-Christian) beliefs and languages were banned. But Iceland remained pagan longer than the rest of Europe. And the old Norse language was still spoken in Iceland even after Christianity was introduced in about A.D. 1000. Sometime thereafter, the Norse mythology was finally recorded in the Eddas.

Thor was probably the most widely respected of the Norse gods. Farmers, in particular, worshipped him. As the god of thunder, Thor was responsible for bringing the rains that watered the crops.

Today Thor is remembered even in America. The fifth day of the week—Thursday—is named after the Norse god.

The name of Thor's hammer—Mjollnir—means "the destroyer." Given that name, it's no wonder that the war-like Vikings often wore necklaces decorated with small hammers.

The hammers of today don't do justice to the power of Thor's weapon. His hammer was similar to a boomerang. After being thrown, it always flew back to the god's hand.

Most modern hammers don't even look like Thor's. His had a short handle on a ring or a cord.

There is an amusing story about why Thor's hammer handle is so short. It seems that the dwarf who was working on it was suddenly interrupted. A fly had landed on his eyelid and stung him, so the dwarf never finished the handle. The fly was really the mischievous Loki, who was trying to keep the dwarf from finishing the hammer.

Dwarfs were master craftsmen who created most of the treasures in Norse mythology.

continued

The dwarfs were very protective of their possessions. If any of their belongings were stolen, the dwarfs usually put a curse on the thieves.

Dwarfs normally lived underground or in caves—and for good reason. Legend has it that dwarfs turned into stone if they went out into the sunlight.

During the wedding in the story, Thor's hammer is put on the "bride's" lap. This part of the story has roots in an ancient Norse custom. Similar hammers were put on brides' laps as the bride and groom made their vows. This act symbolized that the newly married couple had the gods' blessings.

Thor was almost as famous for his beard as for his hammer. In fact, some statues of the god show his hammer growing from his beard.

Men who acted as Thor's priests were called Skeggi. *Skegg* is the Norse word for "beard."

THE DEATH OF BALDER

VOCABULARY PREVIEW

Below is a list of words that appear in the story. Read the list and get to know the words before you read the story.

allayed—relieved; soothed
disdainfully—with contempt; scornfully
dismal—gloomy; cheerless
divine—godlike; heavenly
dominion—land; region
doom—unhappy fate; death
harbor—keep; hide
host—army
hue—color; shade
incantation—spoken charm; spell
inquiries—investigations; questions
invulnerable—safe from harm; unbeatable
mortal—a human
mutable—changeable
ominously—dangerously; fatefully
perplexed—puzzled; confused
presided (over)—ruled; controlled
prophetic—foretelling the future; predictive
threshold—doorway; entrance
unscathed—not hurt; unharmed

Main Characters

Angerbode—a giant and prophetess
Balder—best beloved of all the gods; son of Odin and
    Frigga
Frigga—Balder's mother; wife of Odin; queen of the gods
Hel—goddess of the underworld; Loki's daughter
Hermod—Balder's brother
Hoder—Balder's blind brother
Loki—trickster god; Hel's father
Odin—supreme god
Thor—god of thunder

The Scene

The story takes place in Asgard, the home of the
Scandinavian gods. Action also takes place in the underworld ruled by Hel.

The
Death of
Balder

Odin saw the end of his
world approaching. Step
by step, the gods moved
closer to destruction. But
there was little that Odin
could do to prevent this
tragedy.

The dreams of the gods were often **prophetic.** So when a god dreamt of his own doom, his dream was to be taken very seriously. Frigga,[1] queen of the gods, knew this well. For this reason, she was deeply disturbed by the nightmares of her favorite son, Balder.[2]

Balder was the most popular god in Asgard, the home of the gods.[3] Gods and humans loved Balder. So did all natural things—living and nonliving alike. Balder was adored partly for his fine looks. He was known as the god of light, and he actually glowed with **divine** beauty. But more importantly, he was the gentlest and wisest of the gods.

Frigga met with her husband, Odin. Many of Asgard's

---

[1] (frig´ ga)
[2] (bal´ der or bōl´ der)
[3] Asgard was the home of the Scandinavian gods. Odin reigned as the chief of Asgard and the gods.

other gods were also present.

"We have something to fear, husband," she told Odin. "Our beloved son Balder wakes up during the night screaming with terror. In his dreams, he foresees his own death."

The gathered gods murmured amongst themselves. They were alarmed to learn such news about their favorite comrade. As for Odin, he knitted his brow and hung his head with concern.

Odin knew all about worrisome dreams. He often dreamed of a terrible day in the future known as Ragnarok.[4] This was to be the day of destruction. Ragnarok would come when the good gods fought against the evil gods. According to the predictions, this terrible battle would bring an end to all creation, including Asgard and its beautiful golden mansions.

Frigga's news troubled Odin. It was bad enough that his best-loved son might die. He also worried that Balder's dreams might be yet another warning of Ragnarok.

"This is a serious matter, indeed," said Odin to Frigga. "The two of us must tend to it at once."

"What shall we do?" asked Frigga.

"You are on excellent terms with all natural things," said Odin. "Go to them. Speak to them all. Make sure that none of them **harbor** ill will toward our son. As for me, I'll make **inquiries** of my own."

So Frigga traveled out into the world, talking to all natural things. She spoke to fire and water. She spoke to plants, stones, trees, beasts, and birds. She spoke to diseases, poisons, and creeping things. All swore never to do any harm to Balder. At last the goddess had only one thing on her list—the mistletoe vine.

Frigga found the vine on the eastern side of Valhalla.[5] Then she addressed the plant with a kind voice.

"Little Mistletoe, will you take an oath not to hurt

---

[4] (rag´ na rok)
[5] (val hal´ a) Valhalla was the largest hall in Asgard. The spirits of heroes who died in battle were received in Valhalla by Odin.

Balder, my son?"

The mistletoe was silent. And no matter how many times Frigga asked, the mistletoe made no reply.

"Foolish vine," Frigga said at last. "You're probably too stupid to even understand my words. Well, it doesn't matter. What possible harm could you bring to my son?"

So Frigga returned to Asgard believing that her task was done.

In the meantime, Odin sought the advice of Angerbode, the prophetess of the giants.[6] But it was no easy task to find the giant. You see, she was dead. So Odin had to seek her out in the underworld—the region controlled by the goddess Hel.[7]

Odin saddled his beloved horse Sleipnir,[8] which traveled swifter than the wind. Then he set off for Hel's region.

At the **threshold** of Hel's realm, Odin was met by a ferocious dog. The beast's jaws and chest were red with the blood of the dead he had just devoured. It barked fiercely at the god, but Odin calmly rode downward into the underworld.

The earth trembled beneath Sleipnir's feet as Odin urged him on. At last, horse and rider reached the spot where Angerbode had been buried deep in the ground. Around the giantess' grave stood several tables set as if for a banquet. Fine fruit spilled from golden bowls and goblets overflowed with thick mead.[9]

Odin wondered who the banquet was for. But then he thought he'd better get down to business. He dismounted and began murmuring an **incantation.** As he repeated the spell over and over, a rumbling began deep underground. Suddenly Angerbode rose from her grave, rubbing her eyes sleepily.

[6] (an´ ger bō´ da) Angerbode was a giant female fortune-teller. In Scandinavian mythology, the giants were a race of supernatural beings who existed before the gods appeared.

[7] Hel was the goddess of the underworld. Her region was the home of spirits who died of such things as illness or old age.

[8] (slāp´ nēr)

[9] Mead is a fermented, alcoholic drink made from honey.

"Who comes here to disturb my peace?" she demanded.

Now Odin and his fellow gods were the natural enemies of Angerbode and the other giants. So Odin knew his journey would be wasted if Angerbode knew who he really was. He quickly decided to use a false name.

"I'm Vegtam,"[10] said Odin. Then he pointed to the tables. "That's quite a feast you've got laid out here. Your mead smells fine and strong. Surely you plan to entertain a very special guest. Would you tell me who it is?"

"And why is that any of your business?" grumbled Angerbode.

Odin realized that Angerbode would not cooperate. So he spoke another incantation. This spell forced Angerbode to tell the truth.

"Indeed, I am expecting a guest," said Angerbode against her will. "I'm expecting the god Balder any time now. Ah, I can hardly wait to hear the weeping and wailing of the gods in Asgard! They'll be stricken with grief when their favorite joins me here!

"And he won't go to Valhalla when he dies," continued Angerbode. "No, he won't have the honor of a warrior's afterlife. Instead, he'll come down here and spend eternity with ordinary folk. Oh, that will be a sweet victory!"

"So Balder is to die!" exclaimed Odin. "But how? Who will be the cause of his death?"

"One of Balder's own brothers will do the deed," said Angerbode.

"Which one?" asked Odin.

"Hoder[11] will do the deed," said Angerbode.

"But that's impossible!" sputtered Odin. "Why, Hoder is a gentle god. Besides, Hoder is blind. How could he cause Balder harm, even if he wanted to?"

"Your knowledge betrays you," hissed Angerbode. "You're name isn't Vegtam. You're Odin, chief of all the

[10](veg´ tam)
[11](hō´ der)

gods. And you'll get no more answers from me. What's more, you've troubled me for the last time, Odin. From now on, no one is to disturb my rest—not until Loki[12] is released from his chains."

Odin was more confused than ever. "But Loki isn't in chains," he said. "The last I saw him, he was roaming the halls of Asgard quite freely."

"Nevertheless, my words are true," snapped Angerbode. "Loki won't be released until Ragnarok comes. And now this pleasant chat of ours is over."

With a wave of her arm, Angerbode vanished back into her grave. Odin rode away feeling fearful and **perplexed.** Angerbode's prophecies never failed. But how could this one come true? Could the blind and gentle Hoder kill Balder? And could it be that Loki was in chains?

While Odin was hurrying back to Asgard, his fellow gods weren't sharing his worries. In fact, they were having a fine time. Frigga had told them how she had received oaths from all things.

"Every speck of dust in all of nature has sworn Balder's safety," she said. "I've seen to that completely. Why, you could throw whatever you like at Balder— stones, branches, tools, weapons, you name it. Still, he'd go unharmed!"

The gods rejoiced at Frigga's words. They even thought up a splendid game to celebrate. They stood around Balder and began throwing darts and stones at him. They even struck at him with swords and battle axes. But none of those things hurt Balder in any way. The handsome god just laughed.

In fact, the game was a perfect way to honor Balder. By not harming Balder, all things in nature could demonstrate how they loved him.

But not all the gods were enjoying themselves. The god Loki sat alone, frowning. Loki was a jealous god. And the more he watched the other gods honor Balder,

[12](lō′ kē)

the angrier he became. In fact, evil plans began to hatch in Loki's heart.

"So who cares if Balder is so special?" Loki grumbled to himself. "I bet I can find something in the world that can still hurt our 'beloved Balder.'"

Then the discontented god saw Frigga walking toward her mansion. "Perhaps Frigga knows more than she's telling," Loki said with an evil smile. "Let's find out."

Now Loki had the magical power to change his shape at will. In the twinkle of an eye, Loki transformed himself into an old woman. In that disguise, Loki walked toward Frigga's mansion.

Frigga was surprised to find an old woman standing at her door. "I've not seen you before, have I?" asked Frigga.

"No. I'm not from around here," said Loki. "I'm a traveler, and I seem to have lost my way. But I must say, this is the strangest land I've ever visited."

"Why do you say that?" asked Frigga.

"Well, I just came from a great hall. A number of unusual people there are throwing weapons at one of their companions.

"The poor man is certainly handsome and he must be brave," continued Loki. "But no matter what the others throw at him, he seems unharmed. But how long can he go **unscathed?** Surely they'll kill him sooner or later."

"The man who so concerns you is my own son Balder," explained Frigga. "And he's no **mortal;** he's a god. His friends mean him no harm. In fact, they're honoring him. You see, neither wood nor metal nor stone will do Balder any harm."

"Ah, so that explains it," said Loki. "It still worries me, though. Suppose something poisonous or diseased strikes this son of yours?"

Frigga smiled kindly. "He'll be quite safe," she said. "Neither poison nor disease will hurt Balder. And none of the crawly and slimy things of the earth will harm him, either. I saw to that myself."

"I'm so relieved to hear that," said Loki. "But how did you ever manage such a thing?"

"I traveled out into the world and met with every natural thing—the living and nonliving alike. From every one of them I received an oath that they would do no harm to Balder."

"That's amazing!" said Loki. "Can it be true that *all* things have sworn to spare Balder?"

"Everything," insisted Frigga.

"Without exception?" asked Loki.

"Oh, all but one," said Frigga with a shrug. "There was one little vine that was too stupid and too weak to worry about."

"And which vine was that?" asked Loki.

"It was just a tiny thing that grows on the eastern side of Valhalla," said Frigga. "It's called mistletoe."

"Ah, yes, mistletoe," said Loki. "I know of it. It certainly could do no harm to such a mighty god. Well, now that you've **allayed** my fears, I'll be on my way."

Loki left Frigga's mansion and resumed his godly shape. Without delay he went to the eastern side of Valhalla and found the mistletoe. He removed the berries, leaves, and branches from the vine. When he was finished, Loki held a bare stick in his hands.

Loki grinned with satisfaction. The stick was strong and sharp enough to use as a dart.

Then Loki returned to Asgard, where the gods were still having their games with Balder. Loki saw Balder's brother Hoder standing off to one side, all alone. Holding the mistletoe dart in his hands, Loki approached the blind god.

"What's the matter, Hoder?" Loki said. "Why aren't you honoring your brother Balder like everyone else? Why don't you throw something at Balder, to prove how **invulnerable** he is?"

"I would love to so honor my brother," replied Hoder sadly. "But I'm blind and can't see where he is."

"Come, I'll guide your hand," said Loki. "Why

shouldn't you take part in this celebration? You're his dearest brother, after all."

"But I have nothing to throw," said Hoder.

"Here, take this twig," said Loki.

So Loki put the mistletoe dart in Hoder's hand and led the blind god near Balder. Then Loki pulled back Hoder's arm and aimed the dart carefully.

"Now throw!" whispered Loki in Hoder's ear.

Hoder threw the mistletoe dart just as he had been directed. The other gods cheered at Hoder's throw. They cheered, that is, until they saw the dart pierce Balder's chest and strike deep into his heart. In horror, the gods watched as their beloved Balder fell dead at their feet.

The gods looked at one another, speechless. Then they heard an awful snickering nearby. They turned and saw Loki, who was unable to control his glee.

The gods now knew who was responsible for the deadly dart. Every one of them wanted to punish Loki on the spot—especially Thor, the thunder god. "Just wait until I get my hands on you," Thor bellowed.

But the other gods held Thor back. It was not their place to punish Loki themselves. They would have to wait for the return of Odin, their chief.

Odin soon came back from his visit to the region of Hel. He was even more grief-stricken than the other gods to learn of Balder's death. After all, it was his son who was dead. And he knew better than the other gods what Balder's death would lead to.

"So Loki committed this crime," Odin said to himself. "And now he must be put in chains. Step by step, the universe comes closer to Ragnarok."

As for Frigga, her sorrow knew no bounds. Despite her sorrow, she made plans for Balder's funeral. She gathered all the gods together and spoke to them.

"Friends," said Frigga, "it is our duty to send my son safely into the afterlife. But to do this, someone must be willing to face death.

"You all know that Balder didn't die in battle. So he

can't enter Valhalla as he should. It is our duty to make sure he doesn't spend eternity in Hel's **dismal** region. That would not be a fitting end for a god."

"But what can we do?" asked one of the gods.

"We will send Balder's body away on a funeral ship," explained Frigga. "Then someone must travel to Hel's **dominion** and offer the goddess a ransom. She must be persuaded to let Balder return to us. The trip is very dangerous. Hel is Loki's daughter, and convincing her will not be easy. Still it must be done. Who will do this deed?"

Hermod,[13] another of Odin's sons, stepped forward.

"You can count on me," he said. "Balder was my brother. I'll never let him spend eternity in Hel's land."

The gods were pleased by Hermod's gallantry. Odin was so gratified, he even offered Hermod the use of his horse, Sleipnir. Without hesitation, Hermod mounted Sleipnir and galloped away toward Hel's dominion.

Soon thereafter many mourners began arriving in Asgard for Balder's funeral. The giantess Hyrroken[14] came, together with many frost and mountain giants. The wise god Heimdall[15] came on his horse Goldtop. And Freya,[16] the goddess of love, arrived in her chariot drawn by cats.

Still other gods arrived on their horses or in their chariots. One chariot was pulled by a giant boar.[17] The great god Odin **presided** over the whole company, and his wife Frigga stood at his side. Odin's Valkyries[18] and his two ravens were close behind him.

The assembled gods built a funeral pyre[19] on Balder's mighty ship, Ringhorn. Then they placed Balder's body atop the pyre.

[13](här´ mod)
[14](hērō´ kin)
[15](häm´ dal)
[16](frä´ ah)
[17]A boar is a large and often dangerous wild pig.
[18](val kir´ ē *or* val kī´ rē) Valkyries were female servants of Odin who rode into battles to carry the honorable dead to Valhalla, Odin's great Hall of Heroes.
[19](pī´ er) A pyre is a pile of wood used to burn a dead body.

Balder's wife, Nanna,[20] wept horribly at the sight of her dead husband. So great was her grief that she died of a broken heart. In sadness, the gods placed her body on the pyre alongside that of her husband. Then the gods killed Balder's horse and laid it on the pyre as well.

The thunder god Thor stood beside the pyre and blessed it with his hammer. Odin took a gold ring that had been made for him by dwarfs and threw it upon the pyre. Then he lit the pyre.

The ship Ringhorn blazed into the night, carrying the bodies out to sea. As the fiery ship vanished in the distance, a terrible coldness fell upon the world. In fact, winter had arrived in Asgard for the first time.

Meanwhile Hermod traveled on toward the region of Hel. He rode Sleipnir for nine days and nine nights. He passed through valleys so dark that he couldn't see his hand in front of his face. But the bold Hermod and the swift Sleipnir continued on the journey.

Finally Hermod reached a bridge that spanned the river Gyoll.[21] As he crossed the bridge, a maiden appeared and forced him to stop.

"Who are you that makes such noise?" asked the woman boldly. "Yesterday five hundred dead men crossed this bridge, and they didn't make half the noise you are making."

"I am Hermod, son of Odin. I am looking for my brother Balder. Did he pass this way?"

"Yes, he did," the maiden replied. "He has gone to Hel's palace."

"How do I get there from here?" asked Hermod.

"The road you are on leads down to Hel's stronghold. But only the dead are allowed into Hel's kingdom. You have the **hue** of a living person. How do you hope to enter through Hel's well-guarded gates?"

"I'll worry about that problem when the time comes," replied Hermod as he set off down the road.

[20](nän´ nä)
[21](gē ōl´)

In a short while, Hermod and Sleipnir approached the tall, barred gates that guarded Hel's world. A small distance from the fortification, Hermod touched Sleipnir with his spurs and called aloud, "Over the wall, Sleipnir!" With one mighty leap, Sleipnir cleared the barrier.

Hermod then rode Sleipnir to Hel's palace. Once inside, he rode straight to the throne where Hel sat ruling over her gloomy kingdom.

"What do you seek?" asked Hel in a ghostly voice when she saw Hermod.

"Balder has been confined to your dark palace," Hermod said. "You must set him free."

"And why must I set him free?" asked Hel.

"The world has grown cold and dark without his light," answered Hermod. "Balder was the most beloved of the gods. Frigga herself will see that you receive whatever reward you want."

Hel looked **disdainfully** at Hermod. "Was Balder really as beloved as you say?" she asked.

"Nature itself mourns for him," said Hermod. "All things long for his return."

"Then you must prove it to me," she replied. "If all things weep for Balder, he shall return to Asgard. But if one single thing refuses to weep, Balder must stay in my world."

"You will have your proof," Hermod replied with enthusiasm.

Hermod was greatly encouraged as he left Hel's presence. He felt sure it would be easy to demonstrate the world's terrible grief. But before he returned to Asgard, Hermod knew that he must talk to Balder. Hermod found his brother imprisoned in a dark part of Hel's palace.

The two brothers talked throughout the night. Hermod assured Balder that he would soon be set free. He also explained that Balder's brother Hoder had not meant to kill him.

"Thank you for telling me so," said Balder. "I knew

that Hoder would never have killed me on his own. I suspected that Loki was behind the deed."

Balder then gave Hermod the gold ring that Odin had put on the funeral pyre.

"Return this ring to my father," Balder said. "It will assure him that you found me safe and well."

When morning came, Hermod and Sleipnir began the return journey. Once back in Asgard, Hermod told the other gods what Hel demanded. The gods immediately sent messengers to all parts of the earth. They asked every living being—whether plant, animal, human, or god—to weep for Balder. As before, every living thing was willing to honor Balder.

The messengers also asked the nonliving things to weep. And even the stones and metals gave off moisture, just as they do when they are warmed after a frost.

The messengers were sure they had been successful. They thought that everything on the earth had wept for Balder. But when the messengers were on their way back to Asgard, they met an ogress[22] sitting outside a cave.

"We've never seen you before," one of the messengers said.

"No?" replied the ogress. "You must not have looked hard enough. My name is Thok. I've always lived here."

"Well, then," said the messenger, "we've asked all things to weep for Balder. We need your tears too. Surely you'll shed a few for our cause."

"Balder?" asked the ogress, scratching her head. "Who is this Balder?"

"Surely you've heard of Balder!" the messenger stammered with disbelief. "He was the best, the brightest of all gods—the god of light, we always called him. And now he's doomed to an eternity in the land of Hel unless all creation weeps."

"Well, whoever he was," replied the ogress, "I won't weep for him. He means nothing to me. Let Hel keep him."

[22]An ogress is a female ogre. Ogres are hideous giants who eat human beings.

Try as they might, the messengers couldn't change Thok's mind. They returned to Asgard in despair and told the gods of their failure.

The gods quickly realized that the ogress was probably the **mutable** Loki in disguise. They all gathered together and went to Thok's cave. But they could find no sign of the ogress.

Then the gods were certain that this was Loki's work. Loki had doomed Balder to remain in the land of Hel. Furious, they began to search for the evil god.

Odin himself took control of the search. He rose up to his cloud throne above Asgard. From there he could see all the worlds below. Thor took up his hammer and waited with the other gods below. He wanted to be the one to capture the sly Loki.

Soon Odin called down from his lookout. "Loki is hiding on a mountain top. He is building a hut from which he can watch all sides. You'll have to be careful as you approach his hideout."

"Loki's the one who will need to be careful," growled Thor as he led the way to Loki's mountain.

But Odin was right. As soon as Loki saw the gods coming, he turned himself into a salmon. Then he hid deep in a nearby brook. And when the gods arrived, they could find no trace of Loki. They began to think that Loki had tricked them again.

But then one of the gods found a net. It seems that Loki had invented the device to catch fish to eat.

"I wonder," said Thor, when he saw the net. "Maybe Loki has changed himself into a fish. Let's use this thing to see what we can find in the stream."

The gods took Loki's net and lowered it into the stream. Sure enough, they soon flushed out a large salmon. When the salmon tried to jump over the net, Thor caught it by the tail.

"Well, what do we have here?" Thor said with a triumphant smile.

Loki knew there was no escape. So he changed back

to his normal shape. Thor and the other gods took Loki into a dark mountain cave. There they chained him to a rock.

To punish the evil god even more, they hung a snake over Loki's head. The snake hissed and twisted and spat its poison at Loki. When the snake bit Loki, the god would twist with pain. Then the earth would shake.

The gods gloried in their triumph over Loki. But Odin didn't share their enthusiasm. He knew that by chaining Loki, the universe was heading **ominously** toward Ragnarok, the day of **doom.** There was no way to stop events from unfolding. It seemed that Odin could only sit back and watch as his world came to an end.

Ragnarok did come, as Odin knew it would. A great earthquake broke the chains that held Loki. The evil god then gathered a great army of giants and evil beings from Hel. Loki led this awful **host** against the gods. Odin, Thor, and all the fair gods of Asgard were slain. Fire engulfed all the golden mansions of Asgard. The sun sank into the sea.

Only one couple survived the destruction—a man named Lif[23] and a woman named Lifthrasir.[24] Together, they peopled the new earth that sprung from the ashes of the old. And Balder was finally rescued from Hel's world. He became the god of light once more, though the days of the glorious gods were over.

---

[23](leaf) *Lif* means "life."
[24](leaf´ thras ēr) *Lifthrasir* means "desiring life."

INSIGHTS

The Death of Balder" is another of the stories in Norse mythology. To the Norse, Balder was known as the god of light or the White God. He was a perfect god—always good, never evil—and his hair was the whitest of white. In fact, a certain very white flower was named after him. It is called *Baldersbraa,* which means "Balder's brow."

Both of Balder's parents are remembered in the days of the week. *Friday* is named after Frigga. But how we got *Wednesday* from Odin's name may seem confusing at first.

The name actually comes from Odin's German or Anglo-Saxon name—Wodan. The Anglo-Saxons of Germany shared the same mythology as the Norse. When the Anglo-Saxons invaded England between A.D. 400 and 600, they brought with them their language as well as their gods. As time passed, the Anglo-Saxon word Wodansday became the English word Wednesday.

Odin attended Balder's funeral accompanied by two ravens. These ravens kept watch over the world for the chief god.

Each day Odin sent the two birds out to fly over the earth. The birds would return at night to report everything they had seen. In this way, Odin could watch over the entire world. It is interesting to note the ravens' names—Hugin and Munin—which mean "thought" and "memory."

When Balder died, Odin grieved not only for his son, but also for all the gods. For Balder's death was one more omen of the eventual destruction of the world—Ragnarok.

continued

According to some tellings, Ragnarok has already occurred and the earth has been reborn. In other versions, the destruction of the world is set to happen sometime in the future. Here is a version of how the world recovered from Ragnarok.

When Ragnarok came, the world as the Norse knew it ceased to exist. The beginning of the end was signaled by earthquakes, volcanic eruptions, floods, and fires. Then in a final battle, the gods fought their fiercest foes and died. Finally the world shattered and burst into flame.

Despite all the destruction brought by Ragnarok, not everything died. Life was renewed from a tree called the World Tree (or Yggdrasil). This guardian tree of the gods was said to stand in the center of the world.

The World Tree survived Ragnarok in one piece. And safely hidden inside this tree were one man and one woman. This couple set about bringing life back to the earth.

Nor were these humans entirely alone. Though Odin, Thor, and the other major gods were killed in the final battle, Balder survived to become the patron of the new world and its people.

Loki's position among the gods is unique. Both his parents were giants. But for some mysterious reason, the great god Odin swore a brotherhood with him. Thus, Loki was allowed to mingle with the gods in Asgard.

Loki was a mischief-maker, and he caused a great deal of misfortune. But not everything Loki did was evil. He helped the gods get a protective wall built around Asgard. Loki also helped Thor get his hammer back when it was stolen. (See "Thor the Bride," pages 34-50). However, some said Loki was responsible for the hammer's theft in the first place.

The mistletoe that killed Balder held a special place in the beliefs of early Europeans. Some thought the plant possessed magical powers.

Mistletoe is a parasite plant. Instead of putting its roots into the earth, it attaches to other plants and gets nutrients from them. Because mistletoe doesn't touch the earth, some early Europeans believed it was closer to the gods than other living things.

For example, the Celts called mistletoe "heal-all," for they believed it could heal any sickness. There were also special procedures for gathering mistletoe. The plant was never to touch the ground. And it had to be cut on the sixth night of the new moon. Only a Druid—the high priests of the Celts—could cut mistletoe using a golden knife or sickle.

It was thought that special potions made of mistletoe could heal sickness and give good luck. But you had to be careful. If the evergreen ever touched the ground, it would lose its power.

SIEGFRIED

VOCABULARY PREVIEW

Below is a list of words that appear in the story. Read the list and get to know the words before you read the story.

apprentice—student; beginner
avenge—gain revenge; get even
braving—facing; standing up to
conspirators—partners in a plot; allies
decreed—ordered; commanded
deftly—with skill; cleverly
descendant—offspring; child, grandchild, etc.
emblazoned—drew in bright colors; vividly pictured
fatally—in a manner resulting in death; mortally
fickle—undependable; unreliable
hoard—supply; collection
invincible—unable to be overcome; unbeatable
lair—hideaway; den
potion—liquid mixture; brew
reverently—with respect; in awe
torrent—flood; stream
unwittingly—without awareness; unknowingly
ushered—showed the way; guided
vulnerable—unprotected; weak
wielded—handled; used

Main Characters

Brunhilda—Gunther's wife; a one-time Valkyrie
Fafnir—Regin's brother; a dragon
Gudrun—Siegfried's wife; Gunther's sister
Gunther—Brunhilda's husband; Gudrun's brother
Hagen—Gunther and Gudrun's brother
Regin—Siegfried's tutor; Fafnir's brother; a dwarf
 metalsmith
Siegfried—Siegmund's son; Odin's great-great grandson
Siegmund—Siegfried's father

The Scene

Action takes place in and around several castles located
on the Rhine River in Germany.

Siegfried

A magic ring made of gold gives Siegfried great power. And a mysterious maiden trapped in a ring of fire gives him great joy. But the rings of fire and gold only lead him to tragedy.

The metal sword glistened as Siegfried[1] raised it above his head. With a mighty swing, Siegfried thrust the weapon down upon the anvil.[2] The blade shattered into tiny pieces. Young Siegfried stood there with just the sword's handle in his hands.

"It's useless, just like all the others you made," Siegfried grumbled. The **apprentice** warrior turned to Regin,[3] the dwarf who had made the sword. "Why can't you make a decent blade?"

Regin was annoyed. He was the boy's tutor and a master metalsmith.[4] He had made swords for all the country's warriors, including the king. Regin didn't like being criticized by Siegfried, even if the young warrior was the king's stepson. How many of Regin's swords had Siegfried broken now? Regin couldn't even count them all.

"There was nothing wrong with that sword," snapped Regin. "There was nothing wrong with all the others I made for you, either."

"They all broke," said Siegfried.

"Yes, swords do that when you smash them against

[1] (sēg′ frēd)
[2] An anvil is an iron block on which metal is hammered into shape.
[3] (rā′ yin)
[4] A metalsmith is a person who makes objects out of metal.

iron," complained Regin. "You don't know your own strength, you young fool."

Regin was right. For though Siegfried was still young, he was taller and stronger than any man alive. Everybody knew he would be a great warrior someday.

"If a sword breaks against iron, it will break against the flesh of a dragon," said Siegfried. "And you do want me to kill a dragon for you, don't you?"

Regin scowled. "As a matter of fact, I do," he said.

"Well, then," said Siegfried with a smile. "You must fashion a sword that will withstand my test of strength.

"And tell me more about this dragon," continued Siegfried as he rested against the dwarf's anvil. "Where does he live? Why do you want him dead? If you'd tell me more, maybe I could figure out an easier way to kill him. Perhaps I wouldn't need such a strong sword."

"Don't you worry," said Regin as he **ushered** Siegfried out of the shop. "I'll take care of the details. You just prepare yourself for the fight."

"And that's all you're going to tell me?" asked Siegfried.

"Yes," replied Regin. "I have no more to say until you're armed and ready. Now go. Your training is over for today."

"It looks like I'll have to go elsewhere to find a sword," said Siegfried as he wandered back to the palace. He lived with his mother and stepfather in a castle by the river Rhine.[5] There he found his mother and began to ask her questions.

"You once told me you had saved the pieces of my father's sword," said Siegfried to his mother.

"Yes," she replied.

"Was it really the mightiest weapon ever made?" asked Siegfried.

"It was indeed," replied Siegfried's mother. "Why do you ask about it now?"

---

[5] (rīn) The Rhine River runs through Germany on its way from Switzerland to the North Sea.

"I may have need of such a sword," said Siegfried. "Could you tell me how it got broken?"

Siegfried's mother gazed at her son sadly. She knew the time had come for him to go out into the world. He had reached the age when he needed to make his name as a warrior. So she told him about his father, Siegmund.[6]

"Your father was a hero among warriors," Siegfried's mother began. "Indeed, many thought he was **invincible.** But that belief proved to be false.

"Siegmund was a great-grandson of Odin,[7] chief of all the gods. Odin favored Siegmund by giving him the magic sword of Nothung.[8] Odin promised Siegmund that the sword would never break in combat. But the god proved to be **fickle.** Odin shattered the sword when Siegmund was in the midst of a mighty battle.

"Siegmund was defenseless without his sword," continued Siegfried's mother. "Your father was **fatally** wounded in that battle. I found him before he died, and he gave me the broken pieces of the Nothung sword."

Siegfried's mother opened a chest. She took out the hilt[9] of a sword and the broken pieces of a blade. "Your father told me to give these pieces to you. He said it could be recast into a new sword, which should be called Gram."

Siegfried took the broken pieces of his father's sword from his mother. "I hope I can live up to the memory of my father," he said with emotion.

"I'm sure you will," was the queen's sad reply.

Siegfried took the pieces of the broken sword back to Regin.

"Make me a new sword from these pieces," said Siegfried boldly.

"A new sword from pieces of an old one?" growled Regin. "Such a weapon would never pass your test."

"Just do as I say," demanded Siegfried.

[6] (sēg´ mund)
[7] (ō´ din)
[8] (no´ toong)
[9] A hilt is the handle of a sword.

Grumbling the whole while, the dwarf heated up his forge.[10] Then he recast the broken pieces into a new sword. After he sharpened the edges, Regin handed the sword to Siegfried.

"Now don't go swinging this thing at hard objects," said Regin with a smirk. "It's sure to shatter like glass."

Siegfried ignored the dwarf's remarks and walked away with the sword. "Gram!" he whispered **reverently** as he lifted the weapon. "You're a wonder to behold. Let's see if you're as strong as you are beautiful."

Siegfried raised the shining sword and swung it down against the anvil as hard as he could. Unlike the other swords, Gram didn't break. Instead, the new sword split the anvil in half.

Regin was astonished and pleased. His young charge was definitely ready to become a warrior.

"And now," said Siegfried, "perhaps you'll tell me about this dragon of yours."

"Yes, the time has come," said Regin as he continued to eye the young warrior. "Do you remember when I once mentioned a certain secret treasure?"

"Yes," answered Siegfried. "You said that the treasure had been stolen."

"The treasure has been taken many times," said Regin. "The gold originally belonged to the mermaids who live in the Rhine. But it was stolen from them by a dwarf named Alberich.[11] The treasure was then taken from Alberich by three brothers—the gods Loki, Hoenir,[12] and Odin."

"Odin—my great-great-grandfather," commented Siegfried.

"The very same," said Regin. "Alberich was so angry that he cast a terrible spell on the treasure. Death and destruction are said to come to any who possess it—particularly a magic ring that Alberich himself made from some of the gold.

[10]A forge is a furnace for heating and shaping metal.
[11](all´ber ik)
[12](lō´kē) (hur´nēr)

"The three gods gave the fortune to my father, Hreidmar,[13] because they owed him a debt. But Alberich's curse soon took its toll. My brother Fafnir[14] killed our father and took the treasure for himself. Then Fafnir changed himself into a dragon, and now he guards the treasure."

"And you want me to help you get it back?" asked Siegfried.

"You're a Volsung,"[15] Regin said, "a descendent of Odin and a warrior who knows no fear. Only you can **avenge** my father's death. Only you can rescue this treasure from my evil brother."

"Since you have restored my father's sword, I will help you," replied Siegfried.

Siegfried saddled his swift, gray horse, Grani.[16] The fine horse was a **descendant** of Odin's mighty, eight-legged horse Sleipnir.[17]

"Show me where the dragon lives," Siegfried said to Regin as he mounted Grani.

Perched on a pony, Regin led the way to the dragon's **lair.** Along the way, Regin gave Siegfried several warnings about the dragon.

"Fafnir is very large and fierce," said Regin. "His breath is poisonous and his hide is tough. His saliva will burn you like acid. But if you stab him from beneath, just under his ribs, you can pierce his heart and kill him."

The two soon arrived at Fafnir's hideaway. It was a great, gaping cave near the edge of the Rhine River. Eyeing the situation, Siegfried decided to dig a pit between the opening of the cave and the river's edge. He planned to hide there and stab the dragon when it slithered across him on its way to the water.

Regin watched Siegfried work and rubbed his hands

[13](hrēd´ mar)
[14](fav´ ner)
[15](vol´ soong) Volsung was the name of Siegmund's father. All of Volsung's descendants were known by this title.
[16](gran´ ē)
[17](slāp´ ner)

eagerly. An evil grin spread across his face.

"They'll both be dead soon," he whispered with a laugh. "And all I have to do is watch."

For the truth was, Regin didn't want Siegfried to survive. The dwarf wanted the dragon's **hoard** of gold for himself. He didn't want to share the treasure with Siegfried or anyone else.

So Regin had been careful not to tell Siegfried one important fact. The dragon's blood was hot, like molten lead.

"When Siegfried stabs the dragon, he'll be boiled to death," Regin snickered. "Then I'll be free to scoop up the treasure and carry it away."

Siegfried quickly finished digging. Then he hid in the pit. He didn't have to wait long. The dragon soon awoke, snorting his terrible, poisonous breath. Hissing and twisting, Fafnir slithered out of his den and made his way toward the water. He passed over Siegfried's pit without even noticing the warrior hiding within.

Just as Fafnir's soft underside passed overhead, Siegfried stabbed upward. Gram easily pierced Fafnir's side and tore into the dragon's heart. In a steaming **torrent,** boiling blood gushed out and filled the pit.

Siegfried was scorched by the boiling hot liquid. He coughed and choked and almost drowned. The blood covered all of his body, except for one spot where a leaf was stuck to his back.

But scalded as he was, the young warrior thrashed and struggled out of the pool of blood. Panting, Siegfried lay next to the dying dragon until he could move again. Regin had forgotten that Siegfried was no ordinary man. It would take more than dragon's blood to kill him.

Siegfried sat up and rubbed his arms and his face. They felt different. The dragon's blood had toughened Siegfried's skin so much that no weapon could ever pierce it. Only one spot on his body remained soft—the place that had been covered by the leaf.

Siegfried sat there, trying to understand what had

happened. He lifted just a drop of the dragon's blood to his lips and tasted it. Then he heard a light, musical voice call out to him.

"Greetings, brave warrior," said the voice.

Siegfried turned and looked. The voice was that of a forest bird sitting on the hilt of his sword.

"A bird who talks!" exclaimed Siegfried.

"Oh, that's not so remarkable," said the bird. "Birds talk all the time. People just can't understand them."

"Then how can I understand you?" asked Siegfried.

"You have tasted the dragon's magic blood," explained the bird. "Now you can understand our language. And you can speak it too. This is lucky for you, young warrior. There are few things in this world not known by birds. You can learn almost anything you want to know from us."

"Well, then," said Siegfried. "Perhaps you can tell me more about this dragon and his treasure."

"Indeed, I can," said the bird. "In that cave, among the rest of the hoard, you will find two things. One is a magical iron cloak named Tarn-Helm.[18] The other is a magic ring, made by Alberich himself. It will give you wisdom and power."

"Why didn't my friend, Regin, tell me of these things?" asked Siegfried with surprise.

"Perhaps you should ask Regin," said the bird. "But I doubt that he will tell you the truth. It won't matter, though. You see, the dragon's blood has given you another power. You can hear the truth in people's hearts—even when they lie."

The bird then flew away. Siegfried entered to find the ring and cloak the bird spoke of. The great stash of treasure glittered before his eyes. It was almost blinding. At that moment, Regin came dashing into the cave.

"Siegfried!" Regin cried. "Thank the gods you're

---

[18]*Tarn* is an Old German word meaning "secret" or "hide." *Helm* means "helmet." The Tarn Helm is a helmet that makes the wearer invisible. In this story, the helmet has been changed into a cloak.

alive! I had no idea that Fafnir's blood would boil so!"

But just as the bird had promised, Siegfried could hear the words that were really in Regin's heart.

"Siegfried!" cried Regin's heart. "Why are you still alive? You bothersome pup, I expected Fafnir's blood to boil you to death! I don't much like the thought of sharing this treasure with you—and I won't if I can help it!"

Now Siegfried understood. Regin had wanted him dead all along. Siegfried also knew that Regin would kill him at the first chance. Siegfried drew Gram from its sheath. With one stroke, he severed Regin's head from his body.

And so, in a single day, Alberich's curse did double work. Two owners of the gold had fallen. Fafnir and his brother both lay dead in pools of their own blood.

Siegfried rested for a moment outside the dragon's cave. Several birds sang and twittered in the trees above him. They spoke of a beautiful Valkyrie maiden named Brunhilda,[19] who was sleeping under a spell. The birds said she could be found on a rock high up on a great mountain. The rock was surrounded by a ring of fire. The birds declared that only a truly fearless hero could win the Valkyrie for his bride.

Siegfried listened to this song with wonder. After a while, the birds flew away. Siegfried went back into the cave and gazed upon the treasure. Here was a mountain of gold beyond anyone's imagining.

Even so, Siegfried's eyes easily picked out two objects. One of these was the magic ring. The other was a garment—a loose net of chain mail rings.[20] It was the wondrous cloak called Tarn-Helm.

Siegfried put the golden ring on his finger and fastened Tarn-Helm to his belt. He loaded the rest of the treasure onto Regin's pony and also onto Grani. Even

[19](val kir´ ē *or* val kī´ rē) (broon hil´ da) The Valkyries were female attendants of Odin, often described as goddesses. They rode into battle and watched over mortal soldiers who were fated to die. From these, they chose heroes worthy to meet Odin after their deaths. The Valkyries escorted these slain warriors to Valhalla, the legendary hall of departed heroes.

[20]Mail consists of overlapping metal rings sewn onto leather and worn for protection.

heavily burdened, Grani had no difficulty carrying his master along with the gold.

When Siegfried reached home, he used some of the dragon's gold to decorate himself. He plated his armor with gold, and upon his shield he **emblazoned** a golden dragon. He wanted everyone who saw the shield to know that he had killed the monster Fafnir.

Then Siegfried put the rest of the gold away in a safe place. Now he was truly ready for adventure. He set out to find Brunhilda—the maiden the birds had sung about.

Siegfried traveled far to the south, fighting and performing great deeds everywhere he went. He soon became known as a powerful knight. His magic ring gave him unusual wisdom, and he still carried the magic cloak tied to his belt.

Siegfried **wielded** his mighty sword, Gram, with great skill and daring. His skin, except for the small spot on his back, could not be pierced with ordinary weapons. And Siegfried never told anyone of his **vulnerable** spot. So no foe was able to bring him down.

The warrior also possessed the powers of the dragon's blood. He listened carefully to bird songs and learned many lessons from them. And he could always hear the truth behind people's lies. But he never used his powers selfishly. Siegfried was the perfect hero—both mighty and wise.

Late one day as Siegfried rode along, he saw a great light in the distance. He drew nearer and saw that it was a fire burning high up on a mountain. Grani neighed and stomped, anxious to go toward the light.

"Not yet, old fellow," Siegfried whispered to Grani. "Night is almost here, and it's best to get some sleep. Tomorrow we'll find out what kind of light that is."

Siegfried slept soundly that night and arose early the following day. Then he rode Grani up the mountain.

When he approached the fire, he saw that it formed a towering wall of flame as high as a castle.

Siegfried rode along the edge of the fire, but the flames formed a huge and perfect circle. The blaze behaved most strangely. It seemed rooted and fixed, neither spreading out nor dying down.

"This must be the place the birds sang about," murmured Siegfried with amazement. "Within this circle of flame Brunhilda lies in enchanted sleep."

Siegfried sat in Grani's saddle, staring at the flames. The fire roared and crackled endlessly. He could feel the heat and smell the smoke. But Grani pawed the ground and stomped, eager to go forward into the fire.

"Well, my friend," Siegfried said to his horse, "if you're not afraid, neither am I."

Siegfried urged Grani ahead. With a mighty leap, Grani plunged through the wall of flame. The bold warrior and the powerful horse passed through the fire without harm. They found themselves inside the circle, where Siegfried saw a figure lying on a rock.

The figure was dressed in armor and lay partly hidden under a shield. Nearby stood a war-horse. The horse was completely outfitted as if ready for battle.

"What's this?" Siegfried grumbled to Grani. "I was expecting a gorgeous maiden, not some sleeping warrior. Well, enough of this. We might as well go back."

But the horse shifted and grunted, as if insisting that Siegfried dismount. Siegfried did so and crept toward the strange figure. He lifted up the shield and took off the warrior's helmet.

To Siegfried's surprise, he saw that the warrior was a woman. But this woman was taller and stronger than most warriors. At the same time, she was more beautiful than any woman Siegfried had ever seen.

"This must be Brunhilda," Siegfried whispered to himself. "She's dressed in her Valkyrie armor."

As Siegfried gazed upon the sleeping Valkyrie, color returned to her splendidly shaped cheeks. But she continued to sleep on. Siegfried bent down and kissed her lips.

Suddenly the flames encircling the rock died away. Brunhilda stirred and opened her eyes. When she saw Siegfried bending over her, she didn't seem surprised. She sat up and spoke to him.

"Welcome, brave knight," said Brunhilda.

"Greetings, beautiful Brunhilda," said Siegfried.

"You must be a Volsung," said Brunhilda. "No one else could have come through the circle of flame and awakened me. In fact, you must be Siegfried—Siegmund's son."

"How do you know all this?" asked Siegfried with wonder.

"Through magic, I suppose," said Brunhilda with a shrug. "The same way you understand the speech of birds."

"How did you come to be asleep upon this rock?" asked Siegfried. "And why is a beautiful maiden like you dressed in the armor of a warrior?"

"I was once a Valkyrie," said Brunhilda. "I rode onto the battlefields in search of fallen warriors. I carried the bravest of the dead to Odin's hall of heroes—Valhalla.[21] But during one battle, I disobeyed Odin. He had **decreed** that a certain warrior was to die. But I tried to help the warrior escape."

"And who was that warrior?" asked Siegfried.

"He was Siegmund, your father," said Brunhilda. "Odin was angry with me, so he took away my powers. But Odin also took pity on me. He transformed me into a mortal woman.

"Then he created a ring of fire to guard me. Only a knight worthy of my love could pass through that fire. And I could only be awakened by a warrior without fear."

Brunhilda looked deeply into Siegfried's eyes. "You must be without fear and so...worthy of my love."

Brunhilda mounted her horse, and Siegfried mounted Grani. The couple passed over the smoldering earth

[21](val hal´ a)

where the magic fire had recently burned. Then they rode down the mountain, talking and laughing all the way.

As they rode along, Brunhilda and Siegfried told each other all their dreams, hopes, and secrets. Brunhilda taught Siegfried much about the wisdom of the gods.

They realized how well matched they were in courage and beauty. Finding such a man made Brunhilda less sad about becoming mortal. Finding such a woman made Siegfried glad he had overcome so many difficulties along the way. Soon the two pledged their love to one another and agreed to marry.

"How soon should we marry, Brunhilda?" asked Siegfried as they rode along.

"How soon do you want to marry?" asked Brunhilda.

Siegfried thought a moment before replying. "Brunhilda, you know that I adore you," he said cautiously. "I want us to always be together. But..."

"But what?" asked Brunhilda.

"But I'm young," said Siegfried. "I am a warrior. I need more time to find adventure and fame. Do you understand?"

Brunhilda smiled sweetly. "You forget who you're talking to," she said. "Am I not a warrior, like you? Do you think I want to grow old without **braving** adventures of my own?"

Siegfried was both relieved and saddened by Brunhilda's words. They stopped their horses and looked long into each other's eyes. Without speaking, each knew that they must part. But Siegfried could tell that Brunhilda's love was true. He took off the magic ring.

"This ring is a sign of my devotion," he said as he put the ring on her finger. "Any glory that I earn will be for you. I will never forget our love. I promise that our paths will cross again."

And so, after a kiss, they rode off in separate directions. Siegfried's words were true. Their paths would cross again. But his reunion with Brunhilda would be very different than he imagined—and much, much sadder.

Siegfried continued in his search for adventure, and he found his share. But eventually he started searching for Brunhilda again. Along the way, he arrived at a fine fortress near the Rhine. There he was taken in by a king and queen and their children—Princess Gudrun, Prince Gunther,[22] and two other sons.

The royal couple quickly grew fond of Siegfried and treated him like one of their own children. And Siegfried grew to love Gunther and Gudrun as if they were his own brother and sister.

As it happened, the king and queen wanted to continue their royal line. So they were always looking for suitable mates for their children. Of course, they immediately noticed that Siegfried would make a fine husband for their daughter Gudrun. But there was a problem—Siegfried spoke long and often of his love for Brunhilda.

One day the queen spoke to her husband. "I have a plan," she said. "If it works, Siegfried will gladly marry Gudrun. And Gunther, too, will have a worthy bride."

"What is this plan?" the king asked with excitement.

"Hush," said the queen. "Leave everything to me. I wouldn't want Siegfried to read your heart and learn of the plot. Just stand back and watch."

That evening the queen secretly slipped a magic **potion** into Siegfried's wine. When Siegfried awoke the following morning, he remembered nothing of Brunhilda. In fact, he suddenly found Princess Gudrun very desirable.

Things might have turned out differently if Siegfried could still hear the truth behind people's lies. Alas, the potion took away all his powers of understanding. The birds tried to warn him of the king and queen's trick. But Siegfried could no longer understand their language. He couldn't even remember having been able to talk with birds.

[22](gu´ drun) (gun´ tər)

A few days later, the king greeted Siegfried warmly.

"Correct me if I'm wrong," said the king. "But haven't you been looking at my daughter rather affectionately lately?"

"It is true," admitted Siegfried. "I'm really quite in love with Gudrun."

"This is well," said the king cheerfully. "I can think of no better husband for the girl. I'll be delighted to give you her hand in marriage. But first, I want you to help my son Gunther with a certain problem."

"Consider it done, my lord," said Siegfried. "Your son is like a brother to me. And there is nothing I wouldn't do to earn your daughter's hand."

"It's like this," explained the king. "My son's in love with a warrior maiden named Brunhilda. Have you heard of her?"

"No," said Siegfried. "The name is completely unknown to me."

"Well, it will take a mighty knight to win Brunhilda's love," said the king. "My son could stand to learn from your experience. Perhaps you'd be willing to help?"

"I'd be honored, sir," said Siegfried. "Just tell me what you've got in mind."

"Ride with my son to Brunhilda's castle," said the king. "Then you'll understand your task."

The next day, Siegfried and Gunther traveled to Brunhilda's castle, which was not far away. They were astonished to find the fortress surrounded by a great wall of fire.

Brunhilda had long since finished with her own adventures and had built this castle. She planned to wait faithfully until Siegfried returned. But many knights and princes had sought to marry her. So Brunhilda created the wall of fire to keep such admirers away.

"I will only marry the man who can come to me through these flames," she had declared to all. She was certain that only Siegfried, riding Grani, could do such a thing.

"Look there, Siegfried," said Gunther, pointing to the wall of flame. "Beyond that fire is the lady of my heart's desire. But I can't reach her. You are fearless. Will you ride through the flames on my behalf?"

Siegfried laughed. "I can't understand why you're frightened of a little fire," he said. "But of course I'll go if you wish it."

"Good," said Gunther.

"But you want Brunhilda to think *you're* brave, don't you?" asked Siegfried.

"Of course," said Gunther.

"Then perhaps I'd better disguise myself."

"How can you do that?" asked Gunther.

Siegfried removed the magic cloak from his belt. He wrapped it around his shoulders and pulled it over his head. Siegfried vanished before Gunther's very eyes.

Gunther was amazed. He could hear his friend's laughter, but he couldn't see him. Then Siegfried took off the cloak and became visible again.

"Quite some magic, eh?" said Siegfried. "I won this from a dragon. It does other marvelous things too."

Siegfried wrapped the cloak around his shoulders again. He pulled it up over his head until only his face was showing. Then his features seemed to change. In a few moments, he looked exactly like Gunther. Siegfried laughed again. This time, Gunther laughed too.

So Siegfried, disguised as Gunther, rode Grani though the flames. When Brunhilda saw the familiar horse, she rushed from the castle. She believed that Siegfried had returned. But she stopped in shock when she saw a stranger's face.

Siegfried looked upon Brunhilda's beauty, but his memory still didn't return. He only longed all the more for Gudrun.

"I am Prince Gunther," Siegfried told Brunhilda. "You promised you would marry the man who could pass through the flames to reach you. I have done so, and now you must keep your promise."

"I can't marry you," gasped Brunhilda.

"Why not?" asked Siegfried.

"You're not the man I was expecting."

"Weren't you expecting a man who could ride through flames without fear?" asked Siegfried.

"Yes, but..."

"And aren't you a woman of your word?" demanded Siegfried sternly.

Brunhilda sighed. "I will keep my promise," she said. "I will marry you."

"Good," said Siegfried. "Now we must exchange gifts as tokens of our newfound love."

Siegfried gave her a ring he was wearing. For her part, Brunhilda had no choice. She had to give Siegfried's magic ring to the man who won her hand—the man called Gunther. Little did she know that she was returning the ring to her true beloved. But because of the potion, Siegfried didn't even recognize his own ring.

Then Siegfried, still disguised as Gunther, took Brunhilda out of her castle. Together, they rode through her wall of fire. Once they were outside, Siegfried **deftly** managed to switch places with the real Gunther. Then Gunther returned to his family's castle with his bride-to-be.

When they reached the castle by the Rhine, Brunhilda was shocked to see Siegfried there. But he gave Brunhilda no sign that he recognized her. Brunhilda could clearly see that Siegfried was in love with Gudrun. So she said nothing.

Brunhilda was, after all, a warrior with a keen sense of honor. It was not her way to complain. She agreed to marry Gunther in a double ceremony with Siegfried and Gudrun.

For a while afterwards, things were peaceful in the castle beside the Rhine. If either of the young couples was unhappy, no one could tell it. But one day, Gudrun and Brunhilda got into an argument. It was a silly fight over which of their husbands was bravest.

"Siegfried is the bravest man on earth," bragged Gudrun. "Alone, he killed the dragon Fafnir."

"Gunther is braver," boasted Brunhilda. "He rode through a wall of fire to reach me."

"Don't be silly," Gudrun answered angrily. "Gunther could never do such a thing. He's my brother. I know."

"But he did," insisted Brunhilda. "He rode through the flames to ask for my hand in marriage."

"Haven't you guessed the truth by now?" laughed Gudrun. "You were tricked by Siegfried! That wasn't Gunther who rode through the fire. It was Siegfried in disguise."

"I don't believe you," said Brunhilda.

"Then look," said Gudrun, holding out her hand. Siegfried's magic ring glittered in her palm. "You thought you gave this ring to Gunther, didn't you? But you gave it to Siegfried, who made a fool of you. Siegfried gave you away to Gunther. Then he gave the magic ring to me."

Brunhilda grew pale. It was, indeed, the magic ring from the dragon's treasure. Shaking with anger, Brunhilda stalked away and shut herself up in her room. She paced inside, cold and silent. She wouldn't see anyone, not even Gunther—not until she had worked out her revenge.

Hours later, Gunther talked Brunhilda into letting him into the room.

"What on earth is the matter, my love?" Gunther asked his bride. "Why are you so angry?"

"Perhaps it is *you* who should be angry, my cowardly husband!" said Brunhilda.

"I don't understand," said Gunther.

"No?" snapped Brunhilda. "Well, let me explain it to you. Do you remember when Siegfried took your shape? Do you remember when he came into my castle? Do you remember being too fearful to woo me yourself?"

Gunther nodded shamefully.

"Well, while he was there, he made love to me," lied Brunhilda. She was ready to say anything to get back at

Gunther and to hurt Siegfried.

"It can't be true," said Gunther.

"It is true," said Brunhilda. "Oh, he tricked me, all right—just as the two of you planned. But he tricked you as well!"

Gunther stormed away furiously. Deep inside, he had always envied Siegfried. Siegfried, after all, was brave and powerful, and he was not. So it was easy for Brunhilda to make Gunther believe her lies. Now Gunther was convinced that Siegfried was a traitor who must be killed.

Gunther went to his brother Hagen[23] and told him Brunhilda's story. "But you see, I can't kill Siegfried," concluded Gunther. "He and I have been friends and have sworn loyalty to each other. *You* must figure out a way to do it."

As it happened, Hagen was also jealous of Siegfried's power. In fact, he was anxious to see Siegfried dead, for he had his eye on the magic ring.

"You know, brother," said Hagen, "there's to be a boar[24] hunt tomorrow. We could lead the hunt far away from the castle. No one would see us do the deed."

"Good idea," replied Gunther. "But how do we kill Siegfried? The dragon's blood toughened his skin so that no weapon can harm him. And besides, Siegfried is a mighty warrior. He would surely kill us if we attack him."

"Let me think about this," said Hagen. "I'll find a way."

Meanwhile Gudrun sat worrying in her room. She sensed danger building. She knew that Brunhilda was angry. There was no telling what the warrior-maiden might do. Most of all, Gudrun feared for her husband. She loved Siegfried and wanted to protect him.

Gudrun became so worried that she told Hagen about her fears.

"Don't worry about your husband," Hagen assured Gudrun. "I don't know a warrior in the world who can

---

[23](ha´ gen)
[24]A boar is a large and often dangerous wild pig.

kill Siegfried. Even so, I'll watch over him as well as I can."

"Is there any way I can help you protect him?" begged Gudrun.

"I believe there is," suggested Hagen craftily as he eyed the magic ring on his sister's finger. "You could tell me if he has any weaknesses. That way I'll know what sort of harm to save him from."

"Siegfried has one vulnerable place," explained Gudrun. "He told me about it. A leaf prevented the dragon's blood from reaching one spot on his back."

"It was wise of you to tell me this," said Hagen. "I'll stand at his back to make sure no one strikes him there. But you must mark his vulnerable spot so I can tell exactly where to guard him."

Gudrun agreed. That night, she decorated Siegfried's coat with many new designs. On the back, she stitched the shape of a leaf. As she had promised Hagen, the leaf design marked the spot where Siegfried was vulnerable.

The warriors rode out on their hunt the next morning. In a short time, they cornered and killed a wild boar. They also killed other game—enough for a great feast. After the hunt, Gunther, Hagen, and Siegfried got off their horses and rested beside a brook. Gunther put a potion into a flask[25] of wine and handed it to Hagen. Hagen passed the flask to Siegfried. They hoped the potion would make Siegfried too weak to fight.

Siegfried drank deeply. But the potion had a different effect than the two **conspirators** intended. Suddenly Siegfried's memory returned.

He remembered how he had twice ridden through the flames to find Brunhilda. He remembered how deeply he had loved her. He remembered, too, how he had **unwittingly** tricked her into marrying Gunther. Siegfried was overwhelmed with confusion and sorrow.

Siegfried turned toward Gunther. Gunther could see

---

[25] A flask is a small bottle or container.

by Siegfried's eyes what had happened.

"You betrayed me," Siegfried said to his friend.

"How?" answered Gunther. "Don't you love my sister? Aren't you happy to be her husband?"

"Yes, and I loved you, too, as a brother," said Siegfried. "And you knew how dearly I loved Brunhilda. But even so, you took her away from me. You made me break my promise to her."

Gunther was overcome with shame. He opened his mouth to beg Siegfried's forgiveness. But at that moment, Hagen raised his spear. With one powerful thrust, Hagen drove the spear through the leaf on the back of Siegfried's coat. The mighty warrior fell dead. The curse of Alberich had claimed its last and mightiest victim.

The brothers laid Siegfried on his own shield. They called others to help them carry the warrior's body back to the castle. When Gudrun saw her husband's body, she threw herself upon it, weeping.

"How could this have happened?" she shouted at her brothers.

"It was an accident," said Gunther, turning his face from his sister.

"He was killed by a wild boar," added Hagen.

"You lie!" screamed Gudrun. "The two of you killed him! I can see the guilt in your eyes! How can I ever forgive you?"

Hagen and Gunther didn't answer her. They only lowered their eyes with shame and carried the body into the castle courtyard. There they built a funeral pyre[26] and laid the body on it.

Brunhilda joined the mourners and stood side by side with Gudrun. Weeping, Gudrun took off the gold ring and placed it on Siegfried's finger. The brothers lit the fire.

Hagen saw the magic ring on Siegfried's finger and reached out to take it for his own. But Brunhilda reached for the ring first and snatched it away from him.

[26](pī´ er) A funeral pyre is a pile of wood used to burn a dead body.

"You have taken the only man I ever loved away from me," she cried. "You cannot take this too."

Putting the gold ring on her own finger, Brunhilda threw herself onto the burning pyre. The flames leapt up so high that the sky itself caught fire. Even Valhalla— Odin's great Hall of the Heroes—was burned to a smoking ruin. At last, the bodies of Siegfried and Brunhilda were united.

As if in mourning, the Rhine overflowed its banks and washed across the funeral pyre. The swift current quickly swept the lovers' ashes away.

And if you had been below the surface of the Rhine that day, you would have seen a marvelous sight. Giving off a golden light, the ring that had brought so much anguish into the world drifted to the bottom of the river. Up from below, the beautiful mermaids of the Rhine rose to meet it. The ring's gold had been stolen from them long ago. Now the ring, along with its curse, was put to rest. Never again would it bring misery into the world.

INSIGHTS

The story of Siegfried's life is one of the few epic tales left that tells of the great Nordic heroes of Germany. (Beowulf was another of the Germanic heroes. See pages 98-120 for an account of some of Beowulf's adventures.)

Many of the tragic events in "Siegfried" occurred as a result of one crime—the theft of the Rhine gold. This theft led to one death after another until Siegfried himself was killed and the Rhine gold was returned to its original owners.

But this chain of misery was also caused by the high value the ancient Norse placed on family. When a person was murdered or insulted, that person's relatives felt the loss. Only revenge could calm their anger and restore the victim's good name.

Before Brunhilda met Siegfried, she was a Valkyrie. Valkyries were fierce female spirits who accompanied and served Odin. On earth they appeared as princesses riding in armor on horseback.

Valkyrie means "chooser of the slain." The chief duty of Valkyries was to go to the battlefields and decide (at Odin's orders) who should live or die.

The Valkyries then picked the bravest of the dead and brought them back to Odin's hall. The hall was called *Valhalla,* or "Hall of the Slain."

Odin had a reason for having the dead warriors brought to him. He needed them to be on the gods' side when Ragnarok occurred. (Ragnarok was the final battle between the gods and their enemies.)

When the dead warriors reached Valhalla, they were brought back to life. Every day the lucky heroes ate the flesh of Schrimnir, a marvelous boar. And though Schrimnir was fed to the heroes every morning, the boar magically became whole again every night.

When the brave warriors weren't eating, they were fighting each other. Every day they cut each other to pieces on the practice field. But by mealtime, their wounds were healed and they returned to eat of Schrimnir again. In this manner, Odin kept his fighters in shape for the final battle.

Warriors often called on Odin for help during battle. Some even fought without armor, believing they were under Odin's protection.

One tradition held that it was lucky to be the first to hurl a spear over the advancing enemy. This brought Odin's protection and a sure victory.

Not that Odin was always true to those he favored. Sometimes he switched sides during a battle, just when victory seemed near.

Though Odin may not have been trustworthy, people respected him enough to make many sacrifices to him. Some of those sacrifices were human. Victims were usually strangled and then stabbed with a spear. Often a victim's body was left to hang from a tree for days.

Not even members of royalty were safe from this practice. In Sweden, if a harvest failed or disease broke out, people sacrificed their king as an offering to the gods.

BEOWULF

VOCABULARY PREVIEW

Below is a list of words that appear in the story. Read the list and get to know the words before you read the story.

bolted—moved quickly; dashed
commotion—noisy confusion; disturbance
defiantly—stubbornly; boldly
fancies—fantasies; made-up stories
fiendish—devilish; cruel
fitted (out)—got ready; supplied
hailed—saluted; praised
hearth—fireplace
insolent—insulting; rude
lavished—gave generously; bestowed
plagued—troubled; bothered
provoked—annoyed; angered
reeled—staggered; swayed
resolve—willpower; determination
reveled—danced for joy; rejoiced
scores—a large number; many
scrutinized—studied; examined
subjects—those ruled by a king or queen; vassals
successor—replacement; inheritor; next in line to a
   throne, title, or office
venom—poison

Main Characters

Beowulf—King Higelac's nephew
Grendel—monster; offspring of Cain
King Higelac—king of the Geats
King Hrothgar—king of Denmark
Wiglaf—Beowulf's helper
She-monster—Grendel's mother

The Scene

The story begins in the castle Heorot in Denmark. Beowulf and his warriors then journey to the land of the Geats in southern Sweden.

Beowulf

Above all things, warriors of old sought fame. They wanted songs to be sung about them long after they died. And they hoped that great monuments would be built in their memory. Hear the story of one such warrior.

In the cold North lived a group of warriors called the Geats.[1] The Geats were ruled by King Higelac,[2] a mighty warrior in his day. But the king was growing old. So he looked to the younger Geats to see if they would live up to the warrior way of life.

One day a minstrel[3] came to the Geats from across the water. All the warriors gathered at King Higelac's castle to hear the singer's tales of mighty deeds.

A great fire warmed the hall, and the great Geatish heroes sat eating and drinking when the minstrel began to sing.

Come gather and hear my song
Of sorrow and gloom in faraway Heorot—[4]
In Denmark where brave warriors moan.
For Grendel[5] the evil one who walks alone
Devours the best of King Hrothgar's[6] land.
Grendel yet lives—a horror to all who still stand.

---

[1] (gēts *or* gā´ əts) The Geats were a group of people who lived in southern Sweden.

[2] (hig´ e lac)

[3] A minstrel was a medieval harp player and singer who told heroic stories.

[4] (hā o rot´) *Heorot* is an Anglo-Saxon word that means "deer" or "hart" in Old English or Anglo-Saxon. Heorot was a castle ruled by the Danish ruler King Hrothgar. It is also known as the Hall of the Hart.

[5] (gren´ del)

[6] (hroth´ gar)

"Stop the music!" called King Higelac. "What is this you tell of? Is this just another of your **fancies?** Tell me, poet, what are you singing about?"

"I sing the truth, I'm sorry to say," the minstrel said to the king. "An evil monster called Grendel has robbed Heorot—the great Hall of the Hart—of its finest warriors. I have seen King Hrothgar myself. He is overcome with sorrow."

"This is indeed sad news," said Higelac shaking his head. "The Danes[7] are our friends. And they are brave fighters. Have none of the Danish warriors been able to face this Grendel?" he asked the minstrel.

The minstrel lowered his head. "The greatest of King Hrothgar's companions have fallen to the beast. Just a handful are left," said the minstrel.

The great hall of King Higelac fell into silence at the minstrel's sad words. The only sound was the snapping of the fire in the **hearth.**

Suddenly a huge warrior stood up and faced King Higelac. With a mighty blow the warrior hit the heavy table in front of him. "I've heard enough talk!" he thundered. "I, Beowulf, will not stand by as our Danish friends are destroyed by a monster."

King Higelac smiled inwardly at the warrior's words. Beowulf was his favorite nephew. Indeed, Beowulf was the most powerful Geatish warrior.

But King Higelac made himself frown. He wanted to test his nephew's **resolve.** "What are you saying, nephew? Are you saying that you have a better chance of killing this monster than all the warriors of Denmark?"

"I don't care about my chances!" replied Beowulf. "This Grendel may be able to eat me alive. But that won't stop me. The world must know that the Geats don't let their friends down without a fight.

"I will sail tomorrow for Denmark," Beowulf added. "Any fighter who's not afraid of adventure—or death— can join me."

---

[7] Danes are people who live in Denmark.

With these words, all the other warriors in the hall stood up and **hailed** Beowulf. King Higelac smiled down on his nephew. The king knew that even if he wanted to, there would be no way to stop Beowulf.

The next morning a crowd gathered to say farewell to Beowulf and his companions. Fourteen brave and sea-soned champions had agreed to travel with the famous warrior. Beowulf himself had **fitted** out the ship for the voyage. His warriors stowed their armor and weapons in the ship's hold.[8] They wore their mail shirts[9] and kept their helmets near at hand.

When all was ready, Beowulf stood on the prow[10] of the ship and spoke to his admirers on shore. "We have chosen to face a **fiendish** monster. You may not see us again in this life. But be sure that if the poets sing of us, it will be for our courage in death, not our cowardice."

After speaking these words, Beowulf cast off for Denmark. With billowing sails, the ship **bolted** across the foamy sea like a flying bird. Soon the warriors saw the cliffs of Denmark.

But Beowulf's ship was being watched from those cliffs. King Hrothgar's guards **scrutinized** the approaching vessel in search of some familiar markings. They galloped their horses down a steep path to meet the incoming ship.

"What men are you?" the chief guard yelled to the warriors in the landing ship. "Why have you come so heavily armed? You've given us no password. Do you have permission to land here?"

Then the guard saw Beowulf rise up among the other warriors. The guard stepped back in amazement. He had never seen such a powerful man before. He didn't know whether Beowulf was enemy or friend. But he hoped he would not have to fight him.

"No one has given me permission to land," said Beowulf **defiantly,** stepping off the ship. "And I don't

[8] The hold is the interior of a ship below deck.
[9] Mail shirts were protective garments made of overlapping metal rings sewn onto leather.
[10] The prow is the forward part of a ship.

know your password."

The guard gulped hard with fear. "Whose warriors are you, then?" he asked.

"We serve King Higelac in the land of the Geats," replied Beowulf.

"And what is your purpose here?"

"We're warriors," explained Beowulf. "So we've come to do a little war."

"With whom?" asked the guard, his fear rising. "Not with our king, surely."

"Certainly not," replied Beowulf. "We come as Hrothgar's friends. We understand a certain monster has been giving him some trouble."

The guard began to laugh nervously.

"So that's it!" said the guard. "You've come to fight the foul fiend Grendel."

"Yes, I believe that's the monster's name," Beowulf answered unsmilingly.

"Go home, my friend," said the guard.

"And why should we do that?"

"Some battles can be won, and others can't. This one can't be won—not by any mortal. No warrior can slay Grendel. This monster has the powers of the devil himself. Save your bravery for a contest where the odds are better."

Beowulf took no heed of the guard. "Thanks for the advice," he said. "Which way is it to the castle?"

"I don't believe you heard me," said the guard.

"I heard you well enough," said Beowulf. "My companions and I will fight your monster—and we don't intend to lose."

"Very well, then," sighed the guard. "You're a soldier, so I take it you know the difference between words and deeds. Take up your weapons, and I'll show you to our King. My men will guard your ship."

The Geatish warriors put on their helmets and took up their spears and polished shields. They hurried along the rough and rocky road to the Hall of the Hart. There

King Hrothgar, old and exhausted, lived in what was left of his once-mighty castle. Hrothgar welcomed the wild-looking travelers into his hall. He was surprised and pleased to see Beowulf among them.

"I knew brave Ecgtheow,[11] your father," Hrothgar told Beowulf. "Oh, it's been many years now. And I met you once, my boy. Yes, it was when you were very small—too small to remember, I suppose. People thought you were a lazy child, and slow. But I could see you'd come to good. I knew it even then. Tell me, what brings you to Denmark?"

"I've heard your castle is **plagued** by a monster," said Beowulf. "I've come to get rid of him, or die trying. Tell me about this beast they call Grendel."

"Some here believe that Grendel is one of the off-spring of Cain,"[12] replied King Hrothgar. "Living with Cain's curse, Grendel hides beneath the earth. He thrives in the darkness and hates the sounds of song and laughter."

"Did you do something to anger Grendel?" questioned Beowulf.

"Not on purpose," Hrothgar said, shaking his head. "Soon after Heorot was built, I invited many guests to celebrate. The song and merriment must have **provoked** Grendel. For that night, the fiend prowled into the castle.

"With a superhuman power born of the devil himself, Grendel attacked my men while they slept. Steel blades were powerless against the beast's evil magic. That night he tore thirty warriors to pieces with his horrible claws. Then he dragged the bodies home to his den and devoured them.

"The terror didn't end that night," continued Hrothgar. "Indeed, it had just begun. The beast began raiding Heorot at will. I built new gates and doors, but

[11](eg´ the ow)
[12]In the Bible (Genesis 4:1-16), Cain killed his brother Abel. For his crime, Cain was cursed by God to wander the earth alone. The people of the Middle Ages believed that monsters and other evil creatures were the children of Cain.

none of them kept Grendel out for long. The monster would just smash through them as if they were made of cloth.

"Heorot once was famous for its beauty," said the king sadly. "Look at it now, a deserted wreck. My people have made sacrifices at their stone altars. But even the gods seem powerless against this monster."

King Hrothgar eyed Beowulf. "So you still want to face Grendel?" he asked.

"Yes," was Beowulf's simple reply.

"I am grateful for your courage," said Hrothgar. "If you succeed—and you *must* succeed or die—you won't go home unrewarded. I'll fill your ship with treasures before you sail again."

That night Beowulf took off his helmet and armor. He lay down among his men on a bed of thick furs. He and his men were in the winehall where many of Hrothgar's warriors had met their deaths.

Soon all of Beowulf's warriors were fast asleep. But Beowulf lay wide awake, thinking about the monster. It wasn't that he was frightened. In fact, he feared dying without honor far more than being killed by Grendel. But sleep wouldn't come until he had made plans for the terrible battle to come.

"I'll carry no weapons," Beowulf decided. "This creature knows nothing of steel. It fights with its own claws and fangs. I shall fight it on its own terms."

While Beowulf lay thinking, the fiend slipped through the night toward the castle. The smell of fresh blood filled its nostrils. But Grendel was surprised to find the castle door closed and barred. He thought the Danes had long since given up trying to shut him out.

Grendel pushed down the door easily. Then he rushed into the hall and looked around. The monster's greedy heart laughed at the sight of the sleeping warriors. His eyes glowed red, as if a fire burned inside them. He was sure he could devour every man in the hall.

Grendel crept up to the nearest warrior. Then he bit

through the man's flesh, killing him instantly. The poor man didn't even have time to cry out.

Then Grendel reached for the next warrior, who seemed to be sleeping soundly. He wasn't ready for what happened next. The warrior grabbed his claw and held it fast. The warrior was Beowulf—who wasn't sleeping at all.

"Were you looking for another sleeping man to kill, Grendel?" hissed Beowulf. "I'm sorry, I just couldn't get to sleep, waiting for you."

For the first time, Grendel found himself in a grip that matched his own. The monster wanted to flee, but Beowulf held on. The walls of the castle shook as the two hurled each other back and forth. The whole building rang with screams and howls of pain—the screams and howls of Grendel, not of Beowulf. No matter how hard the fiend struggled, Beowulf would not let go of his claw. The warrior twisted the monster's arm further and further.

As the two struggled, Beowulf's men rushed to their leader's aid. They raised their swords and struck at Grendel from behind. But their weapons did the monster no harm. Grendel's evil magic protected him from human weapons made of steel. Only hand-to-hand combat could defeat the monster.

Beowulf kept twisting the monster's arm until he heard the bones crack in the creature's shoulder. Then, with a mighty wrench, Beowulf tore the giant arm out of its socket. The monster **reeled** back, bleeding from his terrible wound. With howls of pain he fled from the castle and rushed back to his foul swamp.

Everyone in the castle gathered to see the monster's severed arm and claw. Day came, and more people arrived. People who had feared to come to Heorot for years returned to the ruined castle. Beowulf hung Grendel's bloody arm high up in Heorot's rafters[13] as a trophy.

---

[13]Rafters are parallel beams that support a roof.

"The monster is surely dead," said some.

"But where is his body?" asked others.

Hrothgar's **subjects** followed the monster's tracks through the marshes to the edge of a lake. The water boiled with the creature's blood. No one felt sorrow for Grendel's end. At last, all seemed well in the kingdom of the Danes.

The people danced and sang all the way back to the castle Heorot. The monster was dead, and they could laugh again. They told stories and wrote new songs about Beowulf's brave deed. They sang songs of other heroes too. But they all declared that no greater warrior than Beowulf lived anywhere on the earth.

King Hrothgar commanded Heorot to be repaired, cleaned, and hung with decorations. He ordered a great feast to be prepared. Never had the people celebrated more joyously. Beowulf was a hero.

True to his word, the King gave Beowulf and his warriors many fine gifts. Beowulf received a golden banner, a new helmet, a mail shirt, a sword, and golden arm bands. The king also gave his champion eight mighty horses with splendid saddles. All of the Geats received precious objects made of gold to take home with them.

The soldiers ate and drank late into the night. Finally the King retired to his quarters to sleep. Beowulf and the Geats were given soft beds in a room to themselves. The Danish warriors lay down to sleep in the great hall where the fiend had been killed.

Little did the sleepers suspect that another monster lived beneath the lake where Grendel had finally died. This was Grendel's mother—a female horror. Like any mother, she grieved over the death of her son. Deep beneath the lake, she brooded all alone, plotting revenge. When all Denmark was asleep, she rose up from her den.

The female fiend crept toward the castle Heorot. She broke through the door and found the king's warriors sleeping in the great hall. She grabbed the first soldier she could reach and killed him on the spot. The others awoke and snatched up their swords and shields. They didn't even stop to put on their helmets or their mail.

But this monster wanted no fight. She snatched Grendel's arm down from the rafters where it hung. Then she grabbed up the dead man who would be her dinner. Dodging the warriors' swords, she hurried away and disappeared into the swamp.

The **commotion** woke King Hrothgar, who found Heorot in confusion. Then he learned another warrior had been killed—his dearest friend, in fact. The king shook with anger and grief.

In their separate room, Beowulf and his men had slept soundly through the night. They knew nothing of what had happened. When Beowulf awoke, he went to greet the king.

"Did you have a quiet night?" Beowulf asked the king.

"A quiet night!" cried the king. "Alas, my night was filled with horror. By killing Grendel, you've provoked the anger of that monster's mother. She came last night and killed my dearest friend."

Beowulf looked up and saw that Grendel's arm had been carried away.

"I see we celebrated a little too soon," grumbled Beowulf.

"And what do you choose to do?" asked Hrothgar.

"I choose as I always choose," said Beowulf. "I choose to fight. Fate has already decided my end. If I am to die at the hands of this she-fiend, then so be it. I can only promise to seek her out and fight her, wherever she may hide."

Hrothgar trembled with gratitude. He promised Beowulf more treasures if he could kill Grendel's mother. Then the old king mounted his horse and led Beowulf and his warriors away from Heorot. They followed the she-fiend's trail over rocky hills and narrow paths. At the foot of a cliff near the lake, they found the bloody head of Hrothgar's friend.

The king and the warriors gazed across the lake. Its water still foamed and bubbled with blood. They saw weird creatures swimming about in the water. Scaly serpents wriggled close to the surface. And darker, stranger creatures lurked further below.

The warriors heard a loud hiss above them. They looked up. Two dragons were perched on the cliff top, hissing and snorting and breathing smoke. One of the soldiers blew a war horn, and the dragons hurried way.

Beowulf raised his bow and shot one of the water serpents with an arrow. His warriors hooked the thrashing creature with their spears and dragged it onto the shore. It was a pale, ugly, slippery thing.

"Not the most pleasant swimming companions," remarked Beowulf, putting on his armor. "Still, I've dealt with worse."

"You don't intend to go in there, do you?" asked one of the Danish warriors.

"What choice do I have?" replied Beowulf. "There's not much chance of that monster coming out. My mail should be protection enough—that, and the sturdy helmet your king gave me."

"You'll need something more," said the Danish warrior. "Take my sword."

"What's your sword's name?" asked Beowulf. For in those days, swords had names, just like the warriors who carried them.

"Hrunting,"[14] said the Dane. "It's a fine sword, with poison on its blade. It's never failed a warrior yet."

Beowulf took the sword and thanked the Danish warrior. Then with a short farewell, Beowulf plunged into the lake.

Down, down Beowulf sank through the red-stained water. It was hours before he finally found the bottom. And there Beowulf saw the she-fiend he sought. Grendel's mother saw Beowulf too. She thought it **insolent** of him to invade her underwater world.

---

[14](run´ting)

Grendel's mother struck at Beowulf with her claws. But Beowulf's mail protected him from being torn to pieces. So she carried Beowulf toward her hiding place— armor, sword, and all. Other underwater creatures gathered to watch the struggle. Slimy snakes nipped and bit at Beowulf as the she-fiend pulled him down further.

Before long the slithery creatures disappeared and the water grew cooler. Beowulf began to wonder how much longer he could hold his breath. Then, to his amazement, his face was struck by air.

Beowulf gasped and gulped deep breaths. He saw that the she-fiend had carried him into a huge, dim cavern. It looked like some ancient battle hall, a place where warriors once gathered. The water nearby glowed with a strange, red, fiery light.

Beowulf tore himself free of the she-fiend's claws. He lunged at her with the sword, Hrunting. But Hrunting broke at the first blow. Once again, Beowulf knew that he would have to depend upon his own brute strength.

The warrior and the monster wrestled back and forth across the chamber. She bit through his new helmet and tore at his armor. This angered Beowulf, and his anger doubled his strength. He seized the she-fiend by the shoulder and threw her to the floor.

But seemingly out of nowhere, the she-fiend drew a dagger. She thrust it straight at the warrior's heart. Again Beowulf's mail protected him. But he knew he would soon grow too tired to defend himself. Then he saw something hanging above him. It was an ancient, heavy sword—too huge for any ordinary man to handle.

"I've heard songs of just such a sword," Beowulf realized. "It was made long ago by giants, for their very own use. There's magic in this mighty weapon. No one who uses it can lose in battle."

That sword was Beowulf's last hope. He leapt up and snatched it from the chamber wall. He lifted it high above his head and swung it with all his remaining strength. Then with a mighty thrust, he sliced through the she-fiend's neck, bones and all. Her head dropped to the ground in one place, her lifeless body in another. The magical sword shone with a white light.

Amazed, Beowulf slumped against the stones to catch his breath. The water's red, fiery light turned to a gentle, golden glow. Beowulf looked cautiously around by the light. Still clutching the sword, he followed the wall of the room.

Beowulf found Grendel's dead body in a nearby corner. He struck off Grendel's head with one blow of the sword. Magical though it was, the sword could do no more. Its blade melted away like thawing ice, leaving nothing but the hilt.[15]

In the meantime, King Hrothgar and the warriors stood at the lake's edge, staring into the water. When they saw streaks of fresh blood reach the surface, they were sure that Beowulf had been killed.

"The she-fiend of the deep has killed our hero," they whispered to one another. "The mighty Beowulf is dead."

Sadly, the king and the Danish warriors returned to their castle. Only Beowulf's loyal warriors stayed by the lake to watch for their leader. They hoped to recover his body, if nothing more.

In the cavern below, Beowulf continued to look around. In another corner he saw huge piles of gold and jewels.

"It's a shame to leave it here," Beowulf grumbled. "But after all, a man can only carry so much with him. I'll have to content myself with the hilt of this ancient sword and Grendel's head."

Beowulf took the head in one hand and the hilt in the other. Then he swam upward through the murky water. At last his face broke through the surface. He saw that the lake was calm and cool now that Grendel and his mother were dead.

The Geats were overjoyed to see their leader safe. They helped him take his armor off. Then they put

[15]The hilt is the handle of a sword.

Grendel's head on a spear and set out for Heorot. Beowulf had carried the head in one hand, but no other warriors could do the same. It took four of them to carry Grendel's bleeding head.

The Danish warriors gasped when the Geats marched into the castle. Beowulf led them in proudly. Then he held Grendel's head in one hand, swinging it by the hair. "Behold!" Beowulf said in a ringing voice, "the head of Grendel! The fiend's mother has suffered the same fate. Heorot is finally safe."

Once again celebration filled the halls of Heorot. This time the people were certain that Grendel's terror was over. As King Hrothgar had promised, he **lavished** still more treasures upon the Geats.

The next morning Beowulf and his warriors said good-bye to King Hrothgar and his people. Then they set sail for home. When they reached the castle of the Geats, they gave the treasures they had won to their own king, Higelac. Minstrels sang of Beowulf's latest deeds.

"You carried it off splendidly, brave nephew," said Higelac.

"Are you surprised, uncle?" asked Beowulf with a smile.

"Not at all," replied Higelac, smiling too. "I'm pleased, though. This victory of yours shall make brothers of the Danes and Geats. There will be peace between our countries for a very long time."

King Higelac rewarded Beowulf with land and a castle of his own. Then shortly before the king died, he chose Beowulf as his **successor.** Beowulf humbly took over the kingship and was a good, wise ruler—not warlike, as one might have expected. For fifty years, the country was peaceful under his rule.

But fate did not intend for brave Beowulf to die in bed. Even as an old man, he still had one battle left to fight. This is how it came to pass.

One day a slave ran away from his cruel master. As he roamed the countryside, the slave knew that if he didn't hide he would be caught.

Then he stumbled upon the secret entrance to an old tower by the sea. Creeping through the tower hallways, the slave came upon a room filled with gold and jewels. The treasure had been stored there by some ancient ruler. It had long since been lost and forgotten.

The slave **reveled** in his good luck. But suddenly his joy was turned to numbing fear—he spied a horrible dragon sleeping atop the treasure. The beast had guarded the treasure for three hundred years—not that it did the creature any good. The dragon couldn't spend the gold. Even so, it stubbornly kept watch.

The poor slave studied the treasure carefully. "Just one trinket could change everything for me," he thought. "I could use it to buy my way out of slavery."

So the slave grabbed a single gold goblet,[16] decorated with jewels. Then he stole out of the tower.

Some time later the dragon woke up. It sniffed and snorted, sensing that something was wrong. Then it identified the smell. The dragon followed the trail outside and searched around the tower. Of course, the slave had long since gone.

The dragon went back into the tower and examined the treasure. He immediately saw that the goblet was missing. The beast let out a roar of fury.

Night came, and the dragon left its tower. It flapped its wings, took to the air, and flew across the land. Smoke and fire belched from its nostrils as it soared along. The dragon burned all the houses along the seacoast, killing **scores** of men, women, and children. It intended to kill everything in its path until it recovered the missing trinket. When daylight came, the dragon returned to its tower.

In those days, news of an angry dragon traveled fast. So in a few hours the white-haired Beowulf heard the

---

[16]A goblet is a bowl-shaped drinking glass.

story of the awful dragon. He listened calmly and carefully as his people begged for help. He wondered what had caused the dragon to attack.

"Dragons usually have good reason to strike," he thought. "They come to punish crimes or wrongs. Have I done some ill without knowing it? Am I responsible for the dragon's rage?"

Of course, Beowulf couldn't guess the answer.

His people begged him to send some warrior to fight the beast.

"I'll go myself," answered Beowulf.

The people were alarmed at these words. "But we have only one king," they said. "And we have many warriors. Send one of them. Don't risk your own life. We need you to live long and rule us wisely, as you always have."

"Do I look like some weakling?" growled old Beowulf. "Perhaps you've forgotten my past deeds—how I killed the monster Grendel and his mother. No, I'll let no man fight my battles for me. I'll take care of this beast with my own two hands."

Beowulf called for blacksmiths to fashion new armor. He wanted to wear armor made of steel. He knew that hide or wool would burn away in the dragon's breath.

When all was ready, Beowulf put on his helmet and his coat of mail. He took up his sword and shield. He called his warriors together—young ones, mostly. His brave companions from the old days had long since died. Beowulf and these youthful, untried warriors rode out to meet the dragon. At last they came within sight of the monster's tower.

"Wait here," Beowulf told his followers. "Watch the fight from afar. Don't come near until the battle is done. If I don't come out of this alive, finish the deed for me."

His armor glittering, Beowulf approached the dragon's tower. It was day, and the dragon lay asleep inside. But the creature puffed fire as he snored. The smoke and heat from his breath blocked all the tower's entrances.

King Beowulf let out a roaring battle cry. The dragon, curled up in slumber, suddenly woke up. It hissed and roared as it uncoiled. Its fiery breath scorched the tower stones. Beowulf stood waiting in front of the tower, his shield and sharp blade raised and ready.

The dragon lunged at Beowulf, breathing sheets of flame. Beowulf's shield glowed red hot and melted around the edges, but it held. Beowulf's blade met the dragon's flesh twice. The blows drew blood, and the dragon screamed with pain. But Beowulf's heat-scorched sword cracked and broke in his hand.

The dragon spouted fire and thrashed about with pain. It rushed at Beowulf and forced the old fighter back. Fire swirled around the weakened warrior. Beowulf could feel his flesh roasting inside his armor.

Beowulf's young followers hung back with fear. Many of them ran for their lives, hiding in the woods. Only one young soldier, Wiglaf,[17] kept his wits about him. Furious at his cowardly companions, Wiglaf called after them.

"Have you forgotten who you are?" he cried. "Have you forgotten the oaths you swore as warriors, to protect your king and his subjects? King Beowulf was a brave monster-slayer in his time, but those days are gone. He needs our stronger, younger arms. He doesn't deserve to die alone."

But Wiglaf's companions paid no heed. So Wiglaf alone ran to Beowulf's aid. Waves of fire beat upon Wiglaf's wooden shield, and it began to burn. Just in time, the young warrior leaped behind the fallen Beowulf's steel shield. But Wiglaf's hand was badly burned.

Feeling the support of the young man's shoulder, Beowulf gained new strength. He drew another sword—an ancient one called Naegling.[18] He swung it at the dragon's head. But Naegling broke just as the first sword did.

The dragon charged again. It drove its teeth into Beowulf's neck. Ignoring the danger and the pain in his

[17](wig´ laf)
[18](năg´ ling)

hand, Wiglaf crawled under the dragon. Then he sank his blade again and again into the monster's soft belly.

Beowulf drew his own dagger and drove it into the beast's neck. Together, the two warriors brought the dragon down. Soon the beast was dead.

But this was to be Beowulf's final victory. The wound in his neck was poisoned. The king could feel the **venom** stinging in his veins. Beowulf dropped down on a stone near the dragon's tower. Wiglaf brought him water. He took off Beowulf's helmet and bathed the king's wounds.

"You must not die," pleaded Wiglaf.

"I must, my boy," said Beowulf, with just a trace of a smile. "Fate calls me. My time has come. I have the comfort of knowing I didn't live to disgrace myself. I have never avoided danger, and I have never broken my word. Would you have me die a coward's death, safe in my own bed?"

The king slumped down, and he struggled for each breath. With his last strength, Beowulf removed his own gold necklace and his ring of kingship. He gave them to Wiglaf.

"What shall the Geats do without you to protect them?" asked Wiglaf.

"They have you," said Beowulf. "You are the last of our kind."

Wiglaf was saddened by the thought. He was, indeed, the last of the Geats' great heroes. It seemed too heavy a burden for a young man to bear.

Then Beowulf died, lying next to the body of his final foe. Wiglaf sent a messenger to tell all the Geats that their king was dead. He ordered the soldiers to burn Beowulf's body on a funeral pyre.[19] Finally they built a great tower as a monument to the slain warrior and put all the dragon's treasure in it.

And so ends Beowulf's story. Look for no more heroes like him. Warriors of his kind have vanished from the earth.

---

[19](pī´ er) A funeral pyre is a pile of wood used to burn a dead body.

Where, you might ask, is his tower today with its hoard of treasure? It has long since gone, destroyed by wind and time. But it stood long enough to inspire many songs of Beowulf's great deeds. And songs, unlike towers and treasures, never pass away. You have just heard such a song.

INSIGHTS

*B*eowulf is the only complete folk epic in English literature. An epic is a long narrative story or poem centered on a heroic figure—in this case, the Scandinavian king Beowulf. A folk epic is such a narrative by an unknown author.

The *Beowulf* manuscript was written in Anglo-Saxon, or Old English—the form of English spoken in the British Isles from about A.D. 430-1100. Anglo-Saxon was brought to England by Germanic tribes known as the Angles, Saxons, and Jutes. These tribes also brought with them their stories and mythologies, including the story of heroic King Beowulf.

The story of Beowulf almost didn't survive. In the 1530s, King Henry VIII broke away from the Roman Catholic church. During the troubled time that followed, many monasteries and libraries were destroyed, including the libraries that kept copies of *Beowulf.*

During that era, only religious literature was thought to be worthwhile. As a result, some nonreligious manuscripts were used for such tasks as cleaning boots or polishing candlesticks. Only one copy of *Beowulf* managed to escape this terrible destruction.

War was the main occupation of the Anglo-Saxons. Most of their lives were spent defending their territory or raiding other countries. They even slept with their armor resting next to them.

Anglo-Saxon warriors wore boar helmets. The boar, or wild pig, was sacred to Freya—the Norse goddess of love. It was believed that wearing the helmet would give

continued

good luck and protection in battle.

Not that all they did was fight. Simple pleasures, such as eating, drinking, and receiving gifts, were also important to Anglo-Saxon warriors.

Wergild was an important idea to Anglo-Saxons. Wergild, or "blood money," was the specific monetary value placed on a person's life. Wergild varied according to a person's place in society. And it was paid to the family of the person wronged or killed. If wergild wasn't paid, a feud would likely result.

In some respects, the Anglo-Saxons' religion wasn't very comforting. They believed that the goddess Wyrd, or Fate, controlled their lives. In fact, Wyrd controlled even the gods.

Neither did Anglo-Saxons have a rosy picture of life after death. They didn't even believe there was an afterlife. One could only live after death through fame.

And how were heroes remembered? Their stories were told by ancient poets or minstrels—called *scops* by the Anglo-Saxons. These scops were a major source of entertainment for people, delighting listeners with tales of heroic deeds.

Many scops were actual members of royal courts. However, others traveled from place to place.

THE BOYHOOD OF CUCHULAIN

VOCABULARY PREVIEW

Below is a list of words that appear in the story. Read the list and get to know the words before you read the story.

apprehensively—fearfully; nervously
audacity—boldness; daring
auspicious—favorable; pointing toward a happy outcome
barrage—attack; bombardment
bay—bark
decked (out)—dressed; equipped
destined—chosen; fated
dismayed—troubled; upset
eavesdropping—listening secretly; spying
flustered—confused
frenzy—madness; rage; agitated activity
intrigued—thrilled; enchanted
persistent—stubborn; determined
rouse—awaken; call out of bed
scamp—playful young person; rascal
scoffed—laughed; treated lightly or with mockery
subsided—decreased; stopped
tethered—bound; tied
uncanny—unusual; unreal
woe—great grief; trouble

Main Characters

Cathbad—a druid
Cuchulain—boy hero of Ireland
Culann—a smith; King Conchobor's friend
King Conchobor—ruler of Emain Macha
Mugain—King Conchobor's wife
Sétanta—the boyhood name of the hero Cuchulain

The Scene

The story takes place at Emain Macha, the capital of
Ulster in Northern Ireland.

The
Boyhood of Cuchulain

Was Cuchulain a mortal or a god?
Listen to this story of his boyhood adventures.
Then you can decide for yourself.

As a young boy, Sétanta[1] seemed to be mortal. At least
he was raised by mortal parents. But after Sétanta earned
his hero's name, Cuchulain,[2] many said that his real father
was Lugh,[3] the god of light. Surely, only the child of a god
could become a hero at the age of seven.

Little Sétanta and his parents lived in a great house
made of oak. It was a handsome dwelling on a large plain
in Ulster[4] at the edge of the sea. But even at the age of
five, Sétanta was bored. He couldn't find enough to do.

As it happened, Sétanta's family had many visitors.
Their house was a resting place for people going to the
king's palace at Emain Macha.[5] One after another, visitors would tell of life at the palace.

"King Conchobor[6] divides his time three ways," said
one traveler. "He spends a third of his time watching the
troop of boys play at their war games. Another third he
spends playing fidchell.[7] The last third he spends drinking
ale until he falls asleep."

---

[1] (shay´ dan da)
[2] (koo chull´ in or koo hull´ in)
[3] (loo) Lugh was the Celtic sun god. The Celts (selts or kelts) were early
   European peoples who lived in central Europe and the British Isles.
[4] (ul´ ster) Ulster is modern-day Northern Ireland.
[5] (ev´ in max´ a)
[6] (kon´ chov or)
[7] (fēd´ chel) Fidchell is a board game, probably similar to chess.

"You should see the boys at Emain Macha play at hurling,"[8] said another traveler. "They're so wonderfully strong and fast."

"Three times fifty boys live at the palace at Emain Macha," said yet another traveler. "King Conchobor is the greatest warrior in the land. And under his teaching, those young boys will all be fine warriors too."

These descriptions **intrigued** Sétanta. The more he heard about the boys at the king's palace, the more he longed to join them. He begged his mother to let him go.

"But you're only five years old," laughed Sétanta's mother. "That's much too young to go traveling alone. You need an adult warrior to protect you and to introduce you properly. You'll just have to wait until some Ulster warriors pass by here on the way to Emain Macha."

"But, Mother," cried Sétanta, "it might be months before any warriors pass by. Why, I might be six years old by then!"

"And how old do you think most boys are when they begin training for battle?" replied his mother.

"I don't know and I don't care," said Sétanta. "I'm going to Emain Macha right now."

"And how do you plan to get there?" teased Sétanta's mother. "Do you know the way?"

"No, I don't," said Sétanta stubbornly. "But if you don't tell me, I'll just start walking. I'll take the first road that strikes my fancy. I might spend years lost along the way. But I'll get to Emain Macha sooner or later."

Sétanta's mother sighed. She knew her son was telling the truth. He was a very **persistent** child.

"Very well, then," she said. "But it's a long way north of here. And it's a hard road. You'll have to climb a steep mountain along the way."

She gave Sétanta all the directions he would need. Then the boy gathered up his toy weapons—his spear and

---

[8] Hurling is the national game of Ireland. It is a form of hockey played with a wide stick used to hurl or throw a ball.

shield, his brass hurling stick, and his silver hurling ball. At last his mother turned him toward the north and sent him off on his journey.

It was a long, hard road, just as his mother had said. But Sétanta managed to keep himself from growing bored or lonely. Along the way he entertained himself with his toys.

He threw his spear into the air and then ran ahead to catch it before it hit the ground. He used his hurling stick to strike the silver ball, sending it a long distance down the road. Then he threw the hurling stick at the ball, driving it just as far again.

Sétanta continued north, playing his games along the way. He passed safely over the steep mountain. And after a time he came to the palace at Emain Macha. Just outside the palace, he found the king's famous troop of three times fifty boys. Fallomain,[9] the king's son, was leading them in a game of hurling.

Sétanta wasn't shy. He threw himself into the game. But the new boy didn't know the rules. No child was supposed to enter the contest without getting a promise of safety from the older boys. A young player was usually assigned an older "brother" to protect him in the rough game.

The sight of the strange five-year-old with toy weapons startled the pack of boys. At least one hundred of the players stopped in their tracks and stared at him. All the boys were sons of royalty, and they expected any new player to properly introduce himself.

"Look at this ignorant country kid," said Fallomain. "He dares to challenge us with his toys. He has no permission to be here. Let's give him a lesson in manners. On the count of three, throw your spears. One, two, three!"

One hundred and fifty spears flew at Sétanta. But he fended them all off with his toy shield made of sticks. Then one hundred and fifty silver balls came flying at Sétanta's head. He struck every one of those aside with

---

[9] (fal´ lo mān)

his hands and arms. Finally one hundred and fifty hurling sticks came flying at him. He successfully dodged every one.

At the end of the **barrage,** Sétanta stood unharmed. But a change was coming over him. The young boy's hair stood up straight on his head. A red light blazed like a halo all around him.

One of his eyes shrank smaller than the eye of a needle. His other eye opened wider than the mouth of a goblet.[10] He curled back his lips and bared his teeth.

The battle **frenzy** had come over Sétanta. It was the first time he had felt it, but it wouldn't be the last. The other boys stood frozen, staring at him in fear. Then Sétanta leaped at them, and they ran screaming from the field.

The five-year-old knocked fifty of the boys senseless right there on the hurling field. Then he chased more of them into the palace, where the king was playing his daily fidchell game. One bunch of terrified boys dashed right across the king's fidchell board.

King Conchobor reached out and caught the small boy who was chasing them.

"What's the meaning of this?" the king asked Sétanta. "I don't believe I've ever seen you before, you little **scamp.** Who are you? Why are you being so rough on my boys?"

"They were plenty rough on me when I joined their game," answered Sétanta. "I came from far away to meet them, but they didn't treat me like a guest."

"So why didn't you ask for protection?"

"Protection?" snapped Sétanta. "Nobody told me about getting protection. You see how rude your boys were? They didn't tell me anything! Besides, it looks as though they should have asked for *my* protection!"

Conchobor gathered the boys together and made them promise protection to Sétanta. He also made Sétanta promise not to hurt the others.

---

[10] A goblet is a bowl-shaped drinking glass.

Sétanta was thrilled to be one of the king's troop of boys. He was so excited that he had trouble sleeping that night. Rubbing his eyes, he went to the king.

"I can't sleep," complained Sétanta.

"Why not?" asked Conchobor.

"My bed's all wrong," said Sétanta. "I can't sleep unless my head and my feet are at the same level."

So King Conchobor called a servant to fix Sétanta's bed. The servant placed one block of stone under Sétanta's head. Then he put another stone under Sétanta's feet. In this unusual "bed," Sétanta was able to sleep soundly.

In fact, he slept just a little *too* soundly. He was very tired from all his traveling, and he slept well into the next morning. All the other boys were up and at their games, but Sétanta slept on.

One of Conchobor's guards tried to **rouse** the boy. Without waking, Sétanta lashed out with his fist and struck the guard in the forehead. The mighty blow crushed the guard's skull, and he fell dead on the spot.

When Sétanta woke up, he didn't even notice the dead man. He just went straight to his games. He had no idea that he had killed the guard in his sleep.

"He has a warrior's fist!" exclaimed one of the guards. "It kills by itself!"

"Which one of us will try to wake him tomorrow?" asked another guard **apprehensively.**

"It won't be me, I'm sure," said yet another guard.

All the guards agreed. From that time on, no guard ever disturbed Sétanta's sleep. They always let him sleep as long as he wanted.

The next year, when Sétanta was six years old, King Conchobor was invited to a feast at the house of Culann the Smith.[11]

Culann was not wealthy and didn't have a large house. So he asked Conchobor to bring only a few companions. Conchobor chose only fifty of his warriors to go

---

[11](ku´ lən) A smith is someone who works with metals.

with him.

Before he left, the king went to the playing field to say good-bye to the boys. He stood and watched the game and was again amazed at Sétanta's power and skill. Even when Sétanta played against all the other boys at once, he always won.

"Sétanta, come here," the king called from the side of the field.

"What do you want, my lord?" asked Sétanta, pausing in the game.

"I'm off to a feast," the king explained. "I'd like you to join me as a guest."

The other boys could hardly believe the king was granting Sétanta such an honor. But Sétanta was not impressed.

"I'm in the middle of a game," said Sétanta. "I'll follow you when we're finished for the day."

The king had gotten used to Sétanta's **audacity,** so he went on his way.

Conchobor was received with great honor at the home of Culann the Smith. Then Culann asked the king if any other guests were coming. Conchobor said no. He had completely forgotten Sétanta's promise to follow him when the games were finished.

"In that case, I've got quite a wonder to show off to you," Culann said to King Conchobor.

"By all means, let's see it," said King Conchobor.

Culann clapped his hands. Immediately a huge, savage dog trotted to his side.

"This is my new guard dog," explained Culann. "He's so powerful that it takes three chains and three men to hold him. He obeys only me. I turn him loose at night to guard my home and my livestock."

The king admired the dog. Then Culann ordered the dog to guard the gates. The hound obeyed immediately. He sat on a hill that overlooked the road to the smith's fortress. Meanwhile the king and the smith went to enjoy their feast.

After a time, Sétanta came strolling across the hill to the feast. He tossed his silver ball into the air and hit it with his hurling stick. Then he threw his spear and rushed forward to catch it before it fell to the ground. Sétanta had just picked up the spear when the hound saw him.

The people at the feast heard the hound **bay** wildly. King Conchobor leaped to his feet and cried aloud. "I'd forgotten! Poor little Sétanta is coming. He's only six years old. Surely the hound will tear him to pieces!"

Everyone at the feast rushed outside. Conchobor's warriors ran ahead to save the boy from certain death.

As the great hound sprang at the boy, Sétanta batted his silver ball right down the beast's throat. Then he seized the hound by its hind legs and swung it around. Finally he beat the hound's head against a stone.

By the time the warriors reached Sétanta, the dog was dead. Calling his name, they lifted the boy to their shoulders and carried him into the house. Then they set their new hero on the king's knee.

But not everybody was pleased by Sétanta's victory. The boy soon noticed that Culann looked quite **dismayed.** The boy climbed down from the king's knee and went over to the smith.

"Are you unhappy, sir?" Sétanta asked Culann.

"Yes," said Culann.

"Why?" asked Sétanta.

Culann didn't want to offend so mighty a boy. "Don't get me wrong, young friend," he said carefully. "I welcome you into my house and honor you. But I can't share in the joy over your victory. That dog was my good friend. I counted on him for protection. I needed him to guard my herds of livestock."

"Then I should repay you for your loss," said Sétanta.

"That won't be possible," said Culann. "There isn't another such dog in all the world."

"Did this one ever have a litter?"[12] asked Sétanta.

"Yes," said Culann.

---

[12] A litter is a group of newborn animals, as in a litter of puppies.

"Then I'll train one of the pups," said Sétanta. "I'll teach it to take care of you."

"I'd be grateful," said Culann. "Still, it will take several years for a puppy to grow up. In the meantime, my home and livestock will be without protection."

"Not so," said Sétanta. "I'll do your dog's work. I'll be your hound and guard your flocks and property."

"You will be my hound?" asked the smith in surprise.

"Yes, until the pup I train for you is grown," explained Sétanta. "You couldn't ask for a better watch-dog than I."

"What a splendid idea!" exclaimed Culann. "You are, indeed, every bit the hero people say you are. And you deserve a hero's name. Look here, I've got just the name for you! From now on, you'll be known as Cuchulain—the Hound of Culann."

And so Sétanta won his hero's name. And as he promised, he raised and trained another puppy. Until the dog was grown, he guarded Culann's animals and property. And from that time on, he was known as Cuchulain.

After Cuchulain had finished training the new hound, he went back to Emain Macha. When he reached the castle, he found the king was entertaining a very special guest.

This was Cathbad the Druid.[13] Cathbad was teaching the art of sorcery[14] to one hundred men in the castle. Cuchulain was not considered old enough to be one of Cathbad's students. But he hid in a nearby hallway and overheard many of the druid's secrets.

Cuchulain was listening when Cathbad told his students, "Whoever takes up arms for the first time today will become famous in Ireland. This warrior will be known for his mighty deeds. Stories will be told about him forever."

Cuchulain's heart thrilled to this **auspicious** news. He didn't wait to hear the rest of what Cathbad had to say.

---

[13](kath´ vad) (dru´ əd) A druid was a priest in the ancient Celtic culture.
[14]Sorcery is the study and practice of magic.

He hurried to the king to claim his weapons as a warrior.

"But, boy, you're only six," said Conchobor. "Who said that you were ready to take up arms?"

"Cathbad said it is a good day for me to do so," said Cuchulain.

Conchobor had no intention of going against the druid's wishes. So he gave the boy a shield, a spear, and a sword.

Cuchulain began to use the weapons in practice. But they soon broke under the boy's tests. The king then gave the boy another set of weapons, but Cuchulain broke those too. Cuchulain destroyed fifteen sets of weapons, all in a single day.

Finally Conchobor gave Cuchulain his own spear, shield, and other weapons. Those were sturdy enough to hold up, even under Cuchulain's strength. As the boy was playing with his new weapons, Cathbad came into the room.

"Why is this boy **decked** out in such fine weaponry?" Cathbad asked Conchobor.

"Didn't you tell him to take up weapons?" asked the king.

"No, certainly not," said Cathbad. "A bad fate awaits the warrior who takes up weapons for the first time today."

"Cuchulain, why did you lie to me?" the king demanded.

"I didn't lie," said Cuchulain. "I overheard the master instructing his students. Following his words, I came to take up arms."

"Ah, so that's what happened, is it?" remarked Cathbad. "Well, you should have listened to the rest of my words. For indeed, whoever takes up arms for the first time today will be a great warrior and gain fame. But he won't live long. He'll die very young."

Cuchulain only **scoffed.** "Do you think I am afraid of death?" he asked. "We all have to die sooner or later. If my fame lives on after my death, I don't care if I'm only on this earth for one more day."

So Cuchulain got to keep his new weapons.

A few days later, the young warrior was creeping through the hallways, **eavesdropping** on the druid's teaching again.

This time, Cathbad said that whoever rode a chariot for the first time that day would be famous forever in Ireland. Cuchulain hurried to the king and demanded a chariot to ride.

Conchobor gave the boy a chariot and a driver. But the first chariot broke as soon as Cuchulain tested it by striking the frame with his hand. Cuchulain asked for another chariot, but he broke that one too.

Cuchulain broke twelve chariots that day. Finally Conchobor gave his own chariot to the boy. That one survived Cuchulain's test.

Cuchulain was now ready for adventure. He knew that he was **destined** for fame and glory. But where was he going to find this fame?

Then Cuchulain learned of three fierce brothers who lived on the southern border of the country. These brothers had already killed many men of Ulster. Cuchulain saw his chance. He climbed into his chariot and commanded his driver to take him to the southernmost part of Ulster.

The driver didn't really want to make this journey. He had heard much about the three cruel brothers, and he was very afraid of them. But he was more afraid of what Cuchulain would do if he disobeyed. So he drove without raising any protest.

Soon Cuchulain and his driver reached Ulster's southern border. They looked all around, but the three brothers were nowhere in sight.

"Well, they'll be along soon enough," said Cuchulain with a yawn. "I'd better rest. It's time for my nap."

Without another word, Cuchulain lay down by the river and closed his eyes.

"Your nap!" exclaimed his driver. "You're going to leave me standing guard all by myself?"

"Oh, it won't be too much of a job," said Cuchulain.

"How do you figure that?" demanded the driver.

"Simple," said Cuchulain. "Unless all three brothers show up, it's not worth waking me. If one comes, tell him to go away. If two come, do the same."

"Oh, but that's a splendid idea!" said the driver angrily. "I'm sure these murderous men will go away just because I tell them to!"

But Cuchulain didn't hear the driver's words. He was already fast asleep.

The driver was in a very tough spot. It was bad enough that he might have to face the fearsome brothers by himself. He had also heard how dangerous it was to wake Cuchulain. He didn't much care to get his skull caved in.

In the meantime, the driver didn't have any choice but to keep watch. He unhitched the horses and turned them out to graze. Then he sat down near the river.

Before long, all three of the fierce brothers showed up.

"Who's sleeping by the river?" demanded one of them.

"Just a little boy out for his first chariot ride," said the trembling driver.

"Well, the two of you are trespassing," said the second brother.

"That's right," said the third. "You can't graze your horses here. Get off our land at once."

The driver gathered the horses together and hitched them to the chariot.

"All right," said the first brother. "Wake the boy and ride away from here."

The driver looked fearfully at the sleeping boy.

"But look at him," the driver said to the brothers. "He's sleeping so peacefully! Wouldn't it be an awful shame to wake him?"

All three brothers scowled and put their hands to their weapons.

"Wouldn't it be an awful shame if we killed the two of you here and now?" answered one of the brothers. The others murmured in agreement.

The poor driver didn't know what to do. But then, to his enormous relief, he heard the voice of the awakened Cuchulain behind him.

"What's going on?" Cuchulain asked the driver. "Do we have visitors?"

"Indeed we do," said the driver. "But they're not very friendly. They're asking us to leave."

"We're not exactly *asking,*" said the first brother. "It's more like a *command.*"

The threatening man drew his sword and moved toward Cuchulain and the driver.

"You'd better be careful," the chariot driver whispered to Cuchulain. "I've heard stories about this brother. He's nimble on his feet. He's been known to trick many Ulster warriors by dodging all the weapons they throw at him. Then he kills them when they get tired."

"I swear by the people of Ulster!" replied Cuchulain. "Once I throw King Conchobor's spear, he'll dodge no more. Never again will he trick the men of Ulster."

Then the battle frenzy began to seize the young warrior. Once again, his hair stood up straight and a red glow began to appear around him. He drew back the king's spear and threw it straight and hard. The spear thrust straight through the warrior's chest, killing him on the spot.

Wild with frenzy, Cuchulain leaped upon the body. He cut off the warrior's head and hung it on the front of his chariot.

Then Cuchulain stood face to face with the second brother. This one was larger and meaner than the first. But he didn't approach Cuchulain. Instead, he backed into the river and waited for Cuchulain to come toward him.

Again the chariot driver whispered in Cuchulain's ear. "I've heard about this one too," warned the chariot driver. "He fights best in the water. Indeed, he can walk upon the water. He has tricked many Ulster fighters by leading them to deep water where they drown."

"Never again!" Cuchulain promised. "Watch me step across this river as if it were a puddle."

The boy picked up the sword the king had given him. His madness increased. The red light blazed even more brightly around his head. One of his eyes shrank smaller than the eye of a needle. His other eye opened as wide as the mouth of a goblet.

The boy ran so fast that he rushed over the river as if it were dry land. Then he killed the second warrior with a single stroke. With a shrill scream of triumph, Cuchulain cut off the warrior's head and hung it on his chariot by the other head.

Then the third brother came forward. He was even larger than the other two. And he was angry! Again the driver whispered to Cuchulain.

"I've heard of this one too," said the driver. "He's known for his **uncanny** luck. He's never fallen to any weapon."

"His luck is about to change," growled Cuchulain.

Cuchulain's frenzy increased. He curled back his lips and showed his teeth. He picked up his spear and threw it straight and hard, killing the warrior instantly. With yet another scream of triumph, Cuchulain cut off the warrior's head and hung it, too, on his chariot.

"And now, take us home!" Cuchulain ordered the driver with a roar. "To Emain Macha!"

The driver stared at the boy in amazement. Cuchulain's battle frenzy had not **subsided.** On the contrary, it grew stronger by the moment. Cuchulain's hair bristled and glowed as if on fire. His eyes were wild and fierce. And his lips curled back so that his teeth were bared like a vicious animal.

"**Woe** to all living things we meet along the way!" muttered the driver fearfully. "I'll be lucky if he doesn't kill me before the day is through!"

The driver urged the horses forward and drove Cuchulain back toward the castle. Along the way they passed a herd of deer. Cuchulain jumped off the moving chariot and captured one of the deer. He then tied the deer to the chariot. The animal had to run with all its speed to keep up with the chariot.

Then a flock of swans flew overhead. Cuchulain threw stones at them, striking eight. The birds were stunned but not killed. Cuchulain tied long ropes to the birds and held onto the ends. Like kites, the poor birds were forced to fly along with the chariot.

Cuchulain and his chariot made a weird and frightful sight. He was still wild with rage. Sparks shot out of his red skin.

Behind the chariot the splendid deer dashed along. Above the chariot flapped the eight wild swans, each **tethered** to a long cord. And the heads of the three warriors hung from the front of the chariot. Cuchulain shouted threats and insults at everyone he saw on the way.

Word reached King Conchobor of the wild young Cuchulain's advance on Emain Macha.

"Battle frenzy has overtaken the boy!" exclaimed the king. "He's out of his wits with blood lust. The lad doesn't know what he's doing! He'll kill anyone he meets, friend or foe. If we don't do something to save ourselves, he'll kill us all!"

Then the king thought of a plan to calm Cuchulain. He ordered all the women in the palace to take off their clothes. Then he sent them naked out to meet the warrior. Among the women was the queen, Mugain.[15] As Cuchulain's chariot approached, Mugain called to him.

"Hail, Cuchulain, our boy hero!" cried Mugain. "Welcome home!"

Of course, Cuchulain was **flustered** at the sight of all the naked women.

"Where are the palace warriors?" he asked.

"We are the only warriors you will meet today," said

[15](mu gān´)

Mugain.

Cuchulain turned his head away shyly. At that moment, Conchobor's men leaped out of hiding. They rushed toward the chariot and seized the boy.

Then they threw the struggling lad into a vat of cold water. Cuchulain was so hot from his frenzy that the water immediately boiled away and the vat broke. But his frenzy cooled a little.

Then the warriors threw him into another vat of cold water. Cuchulain broke that vat too. But his battle frenzy faded just a little more.

For a third time, the warriors threw Cuchulain into a vat of cold water. At last Cuchulain's battle frenzy died away. He was calm and peaceful again.

Cuchulain climbed out of the vat and dried off. The queen, now fully dressed, handed him a robe. The boy stepped up to the throne and sat on the king's knee. The king laughed and hugged the boy proudly.

"He's really quite a handful for a seven-year-old!" whispered one of the king's warriors to another. "I wonder what he'll be like at seventeen!"

INSIGHTS

The story of Cuchulain is part of Europe's Celtic heritage. The Celts were tribal people who dominated central Europe and the British Isles in the 6th and 5th centuries B.C. By the 2nd century B.C., the Celtic way of life no longer existed on the European continent. But Celtic culture remained more or less intact in Ireland, Wales, and other parts of the British Isles. In fact, the Celtic literature of Ireland and Wales is one of the oldest in Europe.

However, the ancient Celtic stories were not written down until the Middle Ages. Beginning around A.D. 1100, Christian monks began composing written versions of the myths. For this reason, some of the stories have a Christian flavor.

Cuchulain was an unusual hero in Celtic mythology, at least in appearance. The Celts admired tall people with light skin and hair. Yet Cuchulain was described as being small and dark. His appearance was especially strange since Cuchulain's father was said to be the sun god, who is associated with light, not darkness.

Cuchulain was also unique because he had seven fingers on each hand and seven toes on each foot. He also had a bald spot on the top of his head—where kings could kiss him.

And where does the word *Celt* come from? It may be derived from a verb meaning "to fight." And indeed the Celts were known for being warlike—men as well as women. According to some old Irish stories, women may even have been involved in the training of warriors.

In one way, it was fitting that Cuchulain, one of the Celts' most famous heroes, was the son of Lugh—the sun god.

The sun was a very important object to the Celts.

In fact, the four major holidays of the Celts focused on the sun's relationship to the earth. These holidays were held at the beginning of each season to note the solstices and equinoxes of the sun.

Probably the most fearsome of these holidays—Samain—marked the beginning of winter. The Celts believed that the sun's power weakened at that time. As a result, the inhabitants of the otherworld became angry and dangerous.

The Samain festival was somewhat similar to the Halloween of today. As part of the festival, some townspeople dressed as demons of darkness and death. It was the job of the other villagers to drive them away. Figures representing demons were burned in the town square.

Samain was also the time of one of the Celts' most gruesome rituals. On this occasion, they sacrificed to the gods two-thirds of all their healthy children. They hoped that this gift would ensure that the gods would provide grain and grass needed for survival.

The sacrifice of their children wasn't the Celts' only grisly custom. They also cut off their enemies' heads and nailed them above the doorways of their homes.

Apparently heads had a special meaning to the Celts. Many stone pillars have been found with special sections where heads could be placed.

The religious leaders of the Celts were called druids. But they were more than just priests. These multitalented men were also prophets, poets, magicians, scientists, and doctors.

Druids were the wisest men in a tribe, and they were highly respected. In fact, they ranked next in line to kings and chieftains.

continued

Like many other ancient societies, the Celts believed it was dangerous to call a sacred thing by its correct name. For example, the people of Ulster in Northern Ireland didn't swear by the particular name of a god. Instead, they said something like "the god by whom my people swear."

Yet while the gods' names may have been special and secret, the gods' homes weren't. They lived on earth, just like people.

In the myth, Cuchulain was doomed to an early death because of a decision he made in his youth. When given the choice of either fame or a long life, he chose fame.

According to legend, Cuchulain was 27 years old when he courageously faced death. He was fighting his enemies when their magic overcame him. Knowing the end was near, Cuchulain tied himself to a pillar so he would die in an upright position. In true Celtic fashion, his enemies then cut off the hero's head.

MANAWYDAN

VOCABULARY PREVIEW

Below is a list of words that appear in the story. Read the list and get to know the words before you read the story.

base—low; inferior
bewilderment—puzzlement; confusion
consequences—effects; results
domestic—tame
handsome—sizable; good
idyllic—natural; simple
native—local; original people in an area
outrageous—shocking; shameful
perpetual—everlasting; endless
prestige—high status; dignity
prevail—triumph; succeed
ransom—pay for a captive's release; liberate
reap—harvest; gather
resigned—accepted; surrendered
savory—tasty; delicious
sullenly—gloomily; without spirit
survey—look over; inspect
teeming—filled to overflowing; swarming
unique—one of a kind; different
vermin—harmful or disagreeable animals; varmints; pests

Main Characters

Cigfa—Pryderi's wife
Manawydan—Rhiannon's husband
Pryderi—Cigfa's husband; inheritor of the land of Dyfed
Rhiannon—Pryderi's mother; Manawydan's wife; queen of Dyfed

The Scene

Action takes place in and around the county of Dyfed in southwestern Wales.

Manawydan

Manawydan lost everything—
his kingdom, his friend, and his wife.
Some think that he even lost his mind.
But maybe there was wisdom in his madness.

A terrible war had just ended. It began when soldiers of the Isle of the Mighty[1] invaded Ireland. Bitter fighting had followed.

But who had won this war? No one, really. Its **consequences** had been so awful that victory itself seemed meaningless.

Only seven warriors from the Isle of the Mighty had come home alive. And in Ireland, everyone was killed except for five pregnant women. They were Ireland's only future hope.

Now two of the survivors of the Isle of the Mighty's army sat outside London. They gazed over the great city from the top of a hill. These survivors were Pryderi[2] and Manawydan.[3] Manawydan was sad.

"This war has left me without even a home," groaned Manawydan. "Where can I go for a good night's sleep?"

Manawydan had reason to be sad. When he left for the war, his brother, Caradawg,[4] had been king of the Isle of the Mighty. But when Manawydan returned, he found that everything had changed. His cousin Caswallawn[5] had taken the throne by force.

---

[1] The Isle of the Mighty is another name for the island of Britain.
[2] (pru da´ rĭ or pru da´ rē)
[3] (man´ a wu´ dan or man´ a wu´ than)
[4] (car a dog´)
[5] (cas wall´ an)

"Come now, my friend," said Pryderi. "Things aren't as bad as you say. Why, your cousin is king, even if your brother isn't. Surely he'll grant you a favor—some land of your own, perhaps."

"There's no chance of that," complained Manawydan. "My cousin Caswallawn and I have always hated each other. And now I hate him more than ever for taking my brother's throne. No, Caswallawn wouldn't give me any land. And even if he did, I'd be too proud to take it."

Pryderi thought hard, trying to come up with a way to cheer up his friend. It didn't take him long to propose an idea.

"Look here," said Pryderi at last. "Do you want a bit of advice?"

"I'm certainly in need of it," sighed Manawydan.

"I have just inherited the land of Dyfed,"[6] explained Pryderi. "It's not a rich land, but it's not a poor one, either. My mother, Rhiannon,[7] lives there, as does my wife, Cigfa."[8]

"So how does that help me?" asked Manawydan.

"Well, the truth is, I've never ruled a land of my own. I'm afraid I won't be very good at it. It seems to me you'd make a better chieftain than I."

Manawydan studied his friend's face with interest. "What are you suggesting?" Manawydan asked.

"That we rule Dyfed together," said Pryderi. "I'll keep the title of chieftain, but you'll be the real ruler. That'll solve your problem, won't it?"

"Indeed, it would," said Manawydan with amazement. "But how can you arrange such a thing?"

"Easily," said Pryderi. "I'll give you my mother's hand in marriage. She is a widow, you know, and she's a charming and fascinating woman. True, she's not young anymore, but I think you'll like her. In her youth, no lady was more beautiful. And even now, you won't be unhappy

---

[6] (di´ fed) Dyfed is a county in southwest Wales.
[7] (rē an´ on)
[8] (cig´ fa)

with her looks."

"It's a generous offer," replied Manawydan. "But I'm not seeking territory or power."

"Ah, but remember, my friend," said Pryderi with a smile. "A beautiful lady, a place to live, and my undying friendship will come with this deal. Surely you won't turn all those things down."

"It's not likely," said Manawydan, returning Pryderi's smile. "May God bless you for your kindness."

"You'll accept my offer, then?" asked Pryderi.

"Perhaps," said Manawydan. "But I think it would be proper for me to meet Rhiannon before I claim her as my wife."

"But of course," said Pryderi. "We must go to her at once."

So without further delay, the two friends traveled west toward Dyfed. After a time they reached Dyfed's mighty castle, Arberth.[9]

As soon as they arrived, Pryderi's mother, Rhiannon, and his wife, Cigfa, prepared a feast. It had been a long time since Manawydan had seen such merrymaking and good cheer.

Manawydan sat at the table next to Rhiannon. The two of them talked, laughed, and stared into each other's eyes. The singing and celebrating bustled on around them. Manawydan was enchanted by Rhiannon's beauty.

Later in the evening, Pryderi came up to them. "I see that the two of you have become good friends," he said.

"Indeed, we have," replied Manawydan. "In fact, I think I'll take you up on that offer of yours."

"Excellent!" exclaimed Pryderi.

"And what offer is that?" Rhiannon asked, looking back and forth at the two men.

Suddenly Pryderi felt very uneasy. It was no small thing to give away one's mother in marriage, particularly without asking her how she felt about it. And women in the Isle of the Mighty were as powerful as men. What if

---

[9] (ar´ berth)

Rhiannon didn't like this match?

"Dear mother," said Pryderi cautiously. "I have suggested that Manawydan take you as his wife—with your agreement, of course."

Pryderi was most relieved when his mother broke into a smile. Clearly, she was pleased at this idea. Indeed, Rhiannon thought it best that the wedding take place that very night. And so it was arranged. Before the evening was over, Manawydan and Rhiannon were united in marriage.

The next morning, Manawydan and Rhiannon met Pryderi and Cigfa for breakfast. The two couples were pleased at the fine arrangement they had made. Indeed, they felt as though they had all been friends for a very long time.

Now the people of Arberth wanted to celebrate the wedding. So they began preparing a large feast for that evening.

Meanwhile the two couples decided to **survey** the fine country over which they would rule together. Dyfed was rich in game and crops. The land also produced fine honey, and the lakes and streams supplied **savory** fish as well.

Just before sunset, the four friends found themselves standing on a hill near Arberth. They were surrounded by farmland rich with cattle and sheep. Farmers and their families lived in small but cozy huts scattered far and wide.

And from Arberth came the sound of celebration. The two couples knew that the wedding feast awaited them there.

But this **idyllic** scene of happiness was suddenly shattered. A crash of thunder rolled across the land, and a mist surrounded the four friends. The mist was so thick that they couldn't see one another. Then a white, piercing light blazed through the mist, blinding all of them.

Soon the mist cleared and they could see again. But mysteriously, the countryside had changed. Gone were all the farmhouses and animals. And although the castle still stood in the distance, it appeared to be empty. All the sounds of merrymaking were gone. A deep silence lay on the land. It was as if a great war had swept all life away.

Manawydan, Rhiannon, Pryderi, and Cigfa looked around in astonishment.

"Good God," exclaimed Manawydan. "What has happened to the land of Dyfed?"

The four of them searched the nearby countryside but couldn't find a single dwelling. It was as if no one had ever lived upon the land, much less planted or farmed it. Then they hurried back and searched the castle—every last room was empty.

Fortunately there was a good deal of food in the castle's kitchen. Not knowing what else to do, the two couples settled down in the castle and tried to make themselves comfortable.

The food lasted for several months. Eventually, though, it gave out. Then the four friends went out and hunted for food. There was still plenty of game about. But not another person or **domestic** animal could be found far or wide.

The four companions passed the next two years pleasantly enough. But at last they grew bored and irritable with one another.

"Look here," Manawydan said to the others. "We'll drive ourselves crazy if we don't talk to somebody else. I say it's high time we make some new friends. Let's head for a city. We can earn our living there through some craft or other."

So the four of them set out to the east and came to the town of Henffordd.[10] Henffordd bustled with people and offered a welcome change to the four friends. So they decided to stay there and make saddles for a living.

Manawydan was the most skillful of the group—a master of many crafts. He had long ago learned to color

[10](hen´ fərd) Henffordd is the present-day city of Hereford in the English county of Hereford and Worcester.

leather. So he designed and made saddles with decorated pommels.[11] He used a secret process to dye the pommels a sky-blue color. He taught Pryderi to do the same.

Soon Manawydan and his companions were making a **handsome** living. Nobody in Henffordd would buy a saddle from anyone else—not if they could get one from Manawydan and Pryderi.

As it happened, Manawydan and Pryderi were so successful that the other saddlers began to get angry. So the **native** saddlers got together to decide what to do.

"We can't compete with these new craftsmen," said one saddler. "Their work is too good."

"Let's run them out of town," said another saddler.

"That won't do any good," said the first. "They'd just set up shop somewhere nearby. We'd still lose all our trade."

"That leaves us with no choice but to kill them," said a third saddler.

The saddlers were silent for a moment. But soon they agreed to kill Manawydan and Pryderi.

But one saddler wasn't completely sold on the idea. It didn't seem quite fair to him to kill two men for being better saddle makers. So he warned Manawydan and Pryderi of the danger they were in.

"What should we do?" Manawydan asked Pryderi.

"It's simple, isn't it?" replied Pryderi. "We'll kill them when they come to kill us."

"No, no," said Manawydan. "If we fight and kill these fellows, we'll just get in more trouble. Even if we succeed, we'll be put into prison. It's better for us to go to another town. We can earn a living somewhere else."

So the two couples packed up their belongings and went to another town.

"What craft shall we try now?" asked Pryderi as they rode into a new town.

"Let's make shields," suggested Manawydan.

---

[11]The pommel projects upward from the front of the saddle.

"Do you know anything about making shields?" asked Pryderi.

"I saw a shieldmaker at work once," Manawydan replied. "I'm sure we can pick it up with little trouble."

So Manawydan and Pryderi set to work making shields. And, indeed, they learned this new craft in no time at all. The two friends decorated their shields with **unique** designs.

Soon Manawydan and his companions were making a handsome living. Nobody in the area would buy a shield from anyone else—not if they could get one from Manawydan and Pryderi.

But soon the shieldmakers became annoyed with the two new craftsmen. Like the saddlers in Henffordd, the shieldmakers decided to kill off their competition. Fortunately, someone again warned Manawydan and Pryderi.

"What shall we do now?" Manawydan asked Pryderi.

"What we should have done last time," said Pryderi. "Kill the scoundrels before they kill us."

But once again, Manawydan wouldn't agree to kill the other craftsmen. So the four packed up their belongings and went to yet another town.

"What craft shall we try now?" asked Manawydan.

"You tell us," said Pryderi, getting a little tired of all this traveling. "You're the master craftsman."

"Well then, we'll take up shoemaking," said Manawydan calmly. "It's the safest trade I can think of. Shoemakers are gentle folk. Even if we put them out of business, they won't have the heart to kill us."

"But I don't know anything about shoemaking," grumbled Pryderi.

"I do," said Manawydan. "I'll teach you how to stitch. And we'll buy our leather already prepared."

Manawydan bought the finest, smoothest leather he could find. He also made friends with the best goldsmith in town. Manawydan asked the smith to make buckles for the shoes. These buckles were made of metal covered with a thin layer of gold. Manawydan watched carefully until he learned how to make buckles as well.

Manawydan designed the shoes and Pryderi stitched them. Then they decorated them with the golden buckles. Soon everyone in the whole town was buying their shoes from Manawydan and Pryderi.

The cobblers in that town soon realized that their profits were growing smaller. They met together, discussed their problem, and decided to kill the two new cobblers. Again, someone warned Manawydan and Pryderi in time.

"Will you listen to me this time?" said Pryderi. "All we have to do is kill these shoemakers. If we don't, we'll spend the rest of our lives moving from town to town."

Manawydan felt miserable about the situation. But still he wouldn't think of killing the shoemakers.

"I won't take part in any killing," he insisted. "But there's no point in moving on to another town, either. Whatever trade we take up, we'll do it better than anyone else. And when that happens, the rival craftsmen will want us dead. I guess that's just what the marketplace is all about."

"So what should we do about it?" asked Pryderi.

"Let's return to Dyfed," said Manawydan. "I know that we have no friends to go home to. But even loneliness is better than people plotting against our lives."

So the four packed up their things and took to the road again. After a time, they came to the land of Dyfed and went into the castle Arberth. They lit a fire and settled in again.

As before, the four friends took up hunting to provide their food. It was lonely in Dyfed, but Manawydan was right. Loneliness was better than running away from would-be murderers. At least they all thought so at first. But one day, the safe world of Dyfed was disrupted.

It happened one morning when Pryderi and Manawydan took their dogs out for the hunt. Some of the dogs ran ahead of them and disappeared into a small thicket. Suddenly the dogs came rushing out again in great terror. They were bristling with fear, their tails between their legs.

"What on earth could have frightened them so?" asked Pryderi.

"Let's go have a look," Manawydan replied.

When the hunters got near the thicket, a shining white boar[12] charged out at them. The dogs, braver now than they were before, charged back at the boar. The white boar retreated just a little. The savage creature kept the dogs at bay until the men approached again.

Each time the men got close, the white boar retreated. Then it would stand, hold off the dogs, and wait for the hunters to catch up. Manawydan and Pryderi followed the boar until they came to a strong, tall fort. The boar dashed inside the fort, and the hounds followed after him.

"I've never seen this place before," said Pryderi in amazement.

"Neither have I," said Manawydan.

"Could we have missed it?"

"How could there have been a fort here?" asked Pryderi. "We both know this country like the backs of our hands. We would have noticed it by now."

The two stood outside the fort, watching and listening. They heard their dogs barking for a moment or two. But then all was silent.

"What happened to our dogs?" wondered Pryderi.

"I don't know," said Manawydan.

"Well, what are we standing around for?" said Pryderi. "Let's go in there and find them!"

"That wouldn't be wise, my friend," said Manawydan. "This is a magical fort. Otherwise, how could it have appeared here out of nowhere? There's some bad magic at work here."

"How do you know?" asked Pryderi.

"What other kind of magic is there in these parts?"

---

[12]A boar is a large and often dangerous wild pig.

said Manawydan. "Some sorcerer[13] made all our people and farm animals disappear. And now he's put this fort here to trick us. If we go in there, we'll disappear as well."

"But what about our dogs?" asked Pryderi. "No good hunter deserts his dogs."

"It's the only thing we can do," said Manawydan.

But Pryderi didn't agree. Ignoring Manawydan's warnings, he went into the fort. Once inside, he found no sign of the boar or the hounds. Neither were there any traces of people. But something most unusual did catch his eye.

Near the middle of the grounds water flowed from a fountain into a marble pool. Near the edge of the pool, a gold basin hung from four chains. The chains seemed to rise up into nowhere, as if they dangled from the sky itself.

Pryderi was dazzled by the fine quality of the gold. As he got closer, he could see that the basin was beautifully made. He couldn't help going up to it and taking hold of it.

But when Pryderi touched the basin, his hands stuck fast to it. At the same time his feet stuck to the marble where he stood. He tried to open his mouth to cry out, but he couldn't speak. He stood there frozen, unable to free himself or to call out a single word.

Meanwhile, Manawydan waited all day long outside the fort. By late afternoon, he was sure that he would see nothing more of Pryderi or the hunting hounds. Reluctantly, Manawydan returned to Arberth. His wife Rhiannon looked at him strangely when he entered the castle alone.

"What has happened, husband?" she asked. "Where is my son, Pryderi? Where are your hounds?"

"They disappeared," was Manawydan's simple reply.

"Disappeared? Just like that—poof—gone?" asked Rhiannon.

"Well, no, not exactly. You see, we found a strange

[13]A sorcerer is a magician.

fort. First the dogs went inside; then Pryderi followed. I warned him not to go inside because I was sure it was a magic fort."

"And you left Pryderi there?" Rhiannon cried. "A fine friend you've proven to be! Do you think Pryderi would have left you there? No. He'd have gone into the fort to look for you, that's what he'd have done!"

Manawydan hung his head with shame. "You're right, my dear," he said. "I must go back at once and find my friend."

"No," said Rhiannon. "I won't trust a fool and a coward with the life of my son. I'll go myself."

And with that, Rhiannon went out in search of the fort. She soon found it and entered through the open gate. Immediately she saw Pryderi standing at the fountain holding the golden basin.

Rhiannon walked up to Pryderi. Her son gazed at her, his face frozen into an expression of surprise. Of course, he could say nothing.

Rhiannon didn't yet understand that her son was frozen to the basin. She almost wept with joy to have found him.

"Pryderi, my son," she said, "I'm so glad to see you. I thought I'd lost you forever. But what's the matter? Aren't you glad to see me? Why do you stare at me as if you don't even know me?"

But Pryderi remained silent. Rhiannon took hold of the basin to pull it from his hands. Instantly she was frozen just like her son. The two of them stood staring at each other in **perpetual** surprise, unable to speak a word.

The sun set and still the mother and son stood there, unable to escape or speak. As night descended, a mist **teeming** with weird shadows and unearthly sounds filled the fort. Then the two could see nothing at all.

When morning came, the fort had disappeared. Rhiannon and Pryderi had vanished too, just like all the other inhabitants of Dyfed.

The day came and went, and neither Pryderi nor

Rhiannon came home. Cigfa went crazy with grief. Manawydan tried to comfort his sister-in-law, but she pushed him away.

"I don't care if I live or die," Cigfa sobbed. "There were only four of us left in the whole land, and now there are only two. And it's all your doing!"

"What on earth do you mean?" asked Manawydan with amazement.

"Well, it's obvious, isn't it?" cried Cigfa. "You're a sorcerer. You've made everybody disappear but me. Now go ahead and make me disappear too. You'll have the whole country all to yourself."

Manawydan then told her all that had happened at the fort. He told her how Pryderi had gone inside and not come back.

"No doubt, Rhiannon has met the same fate," he concluded. "There's nothing you or I can do about it. Please believe me, Cigfa. I'm no sorcerer; I'm a true friend."

Cigfa dried her eyes. She had no choice but to take Manawydan at his word.

"What shall we do?" she asked.

"Well, there's no use staying in Dyfed," said Manawydan. "Without our dogs, we won't even be able to hunt for food. We'll go east again. It'll be easier to support ourselves there."

Cigfa agreed, and the two of them traveled to a town east of Dyfed. Manawydan decided to be a shoemaker again.

Cigfa didn't much care for the idea. She thought shoemaking was too **base** for a well-born man like Manawydan. But Manawydan was contented making shoes. He was just happy to be busy.

But as before, Manawydan's work soon attracted all the business in the town. And also as before, he learned that the shoemakers were plotting to kill him.

Now Cigfa wanted to kill the other shoemakers before they could kill Manawydan. But once again, Manawydan refused to fight. He insisted that he and

Cigfa return to Dyfed.

Manawydan and Cigfa **resigned** themselves to the fact that they would have no friends back in Dyfed. But the lack of food would be a problem. Without hunting dogs, how could they hope to keep themselves fed?

Manawydan had an idea. Before he and Cigfa left the town, he bought a load of wheat seeds.

Once back in Dyfed, he planted the wheat in three fields. The crops soon began to grow tall and healthy. Manawydan was pleased. If the harvest was plentiful, he and Cigfa wouldn't have to worry about food.

While Manawydan and Cigfa waited for the wheat to grow, they settled into a comfortable routine. Manawydan fished in the streams for food. And although he had no dogs, he learned to kill deer on his own.

True, it was a bit lonely in Dyfed for just the two of them. But it was a beautiful land. And there were no tradesmen who wanted to kill them.

At last the wheat fields promised a handsome crop. Manawydan could see that the first field he had planted was nearly ready to cut.

"Tomorrow morning," said Manawydan, "I'll **reap** that field."

The next morning Manawydan went out to harvest his first field of wheat. But he found nothing but bare stalks. Each stalk had been broken off, and the tops had been carried away. All the spikes of wheat[14] were gone.

Manawydan was amazed. But now he could see that the next field looked even finer than the first. It was nearly ripe and ready to harvest.

"Tomorrow morning," said Manawydan, "I'll reap that field."

The next morning, Manawydan went out to harvest his second field of wheat. But again he found nothing but bare stalks.

"Who could have done such a thing?" he asked Cigfa.

"Who, indeed, unless it's that sorcerer again," replied

[14]The spike of wheat is the cluster of seeds at the end of the stalk.

Cigfa. "We were wrong to come back here. We should have stayed in that town and fought for our lives. How can we **prevail** against the forces of magic?"

"Keep heart, Cigfa," Manawydan said, pointing at his third field. "My last crop looks even finer than the others. I'll reap it tomorrow morning."

"Oh, do you really think so?" replied Cigfa with a suspicious smile. "How silly of me to imagine that our sorcerer might destroy this crop too!"

"Well, what do you suggest I do?" asked Manawydan impatiently.

"It might be smart to guard your field tonight," said Cigfa. "Not that it will do any good."

Stung by Cigfa's words, Manawydan decided to set up guard. So he gathered up his weapons and went to the edge of the field.

Soon night fell and all was quiet. Manawydan had seen nothing unusual. But at midnight, he heard a great rustling noise in the field. Then he saw little creatures scurrying about. He had to stare in the moonlight to see what they were.

"Mice!" he gasped.

Indeed, the field was crawling with little rodents. There were hundreds, perhaps thousands of them—far too many for Manawydan to count.

The mice were attacking the wheat. Each of them climbed a stalk and bent it down. Then other mice broke off the wheat at the top of each stalk and carried it off. Manawydan couldn't see a single stalk of wheat that didn't have a mouse tugging and pulling on it.

In anger, Manawydan rushed into the field and struck out at the mice. But they were too small and too fast for him. It was like swatting at gnats or birds in flight. Then he saw one mouse that was so pudgy it could barely move.

Manawydan followed along behind the fat, slow mouse. Then with a quick grab, he caught the creature by the tail. The mouse squeaked and struggled mightily, but Manawydan was able to lower it into his glove. To make sure the mouse didn't escape, Manawydan tied the opening of the glove shut with a string.

By this time, all the other mice had escaped—along with most of the wheat. So Manawydan took his only catch back to the castle. Then he went into the room where Cigfa was sitting before a fire. He hung the glove, with the mouse in it, on a peg on the wall.

"What's in there, my lord?" asked Cigfa, pointing to the glove.

"A thief," answered Manawydan. "Just one of the criminals who ruined our fields."

"What kind of thief could you put in your glove?" asked Cigfa.

"A mouse," responded Manawydan **sullenly.** "A pudgy and slow mouse that, along with about a thousand other mice, has destroyed our wheat."

"And what are you going to do with this pudgy and slow mouse?"

"I'll hang it tomorrow."

"Oh, that's a brave solution to your problem," laughed Cigfa. "A mighty ruler of great **prestige** hanging a little mouse."

"It's not a laughing matter!" snapped Manawydan. "You should have seen how vicious and destructive they were! I wish I could get my hands on all of them. I'd hang them. As it is, I'll hang the one I have."

"Don't be foolish," said Cigfa. "The last field has been destroyed, and no more damage can be done. Let the rodent go."

"Certainly not," said Manawydan.

"God forbid that I should waste my breath begging mercy for a mouse," said Cigfa with a sigh. "Hang the mouse if it will make you feel better. But you're going to look pretty silly."

The next day Manawydan took the mouse to the hill outside the castle. He pushed two forked sticks into the ground to make a gallows.[15]

[15]A gallows is a frame from which criminals are hanged.

While he was busy doing this, he saw a studious-looking man approaching. The man was reading a book as he walked along. He was dressed in cheap, worn-out clothes. It had been seven years since Manawydan had seen a stranger in Dyfed.

"Good day to you, my lord," said the scholar, recognizing Manawydan's nobility.

"Welcome, Scholar," Manawydan replied. "Where have you come from?"

"From eastern parts, my lord," replied the scholar. "I'm a songmaker. Why do you ask?"

"I haven't seen a stranger in these parts for seven years," said Manawydan.

"Well, lord, I'm just passing through on the way to my own country," said the scholar. Then he looked more closely at what Manawydan was up to. "And what sort of work are you doing, my lord?"

"I'm hanging a thief," replied Manawydan. "I caught it stealing from me."

"What kind of thief, my lord?" the scholar asked in great confusion. "I see something in your hand that looks rather like a mouse. It doesn't seem right for a man of your dignity to touch a creature such as that. Let it go."

"By God, I won't!" exclaimed Manawydan. "I caught it stealing, and I'll treat it like I'd treat any other thief! I'll hang it here and now!"

"Look here," insisted the scholar, "it's bad enough to hang a poor little mouse. But it's quite out of the question to make a fool of yourself like this. I just can't bear to see it."

"How do you plan to stop me?" asked Manawydan.

"I'll tell you what," said the scholar. "I'll **ransom** the creature. I'll give you one pound[16] if you'll let the rodent go."

"No," said Manawydan. "I won't release it, not even for ransom."

"Do as you like, then," said the scholar. "I wouldn't

[16]A pound is a unit of money in England. It is similar to the American dollar.

normally trouble myself. But I find it shameful to see a fine gentleman act with such stupidity."

The scholar went on his way, shaking his head in **bewilderment.** Meanwhile Manawydan began to tie a cross piece to the two forks. But he was interrupted again when a priest appeared, mounted on a horse.

"Good day to you," said the priest.

"And may God prosper you," said Manawydan. "I ask your blessing."

"The blessing of God be upon you," said the priest. Then he looked more closely at what Manawydan was doing. "What sort of work are you doing, my lord?"

"I'm hanging a thief," he replied. "I caught it stealing from me."

"What kind of a thief, my lord?" asked the priest.

"A mouse—or so it would appear," said Manawydan. "Whatever it is, it stole from me. I'm punishing it, as one would any thief."

"But this is **outrageous,** my lord," said the priest. "I can't stand by and watch you hang mere **vermin.** Here, I'll ransom it. I'll give you three pounds if you will let it go."

"Absolutely not," said Manawydan. "The mouse is a thief, and all thieves hang."

"Have it your own way, my lord," said the priest with a shrug. And he started to ride away. "I was only trying to keep you from looking ridiculous."

By this time, Manawydan had finished the tiny gallows. So he tied a string around the mouse's neck. He held the mouse up and began to tie the string on the crossbar. Then he saw a bishop approaching. The bishop was accompanied by several servants and seven horses carrying baggage. Manawydan stopped tying the string and turned toward the bishop.

"Greetings to you, my lord," said the bishop.

"And to you as well," said Manawydan.

"But what on earth are you doing here?" asked the bishop.

"I'm hanging a thief," replied Manawydan. "I caught

it stealing from me."

"But isn't that a mouse I see in your hand?" asked the bishop.

"Indeed, it is," answered Manawydan. "This is the very thief I spoke of."

"Oh dear, oh dear," said the bishop. "I'm on my way home from a hanging as it is. I'm hardly in the mood to see another death. Really, doesn't a gentleman like you have better things to do? Must you go around hanging mice?

"I'll tell you what," continued the bishop. "I'll ransom the creature to save you the trouble and embarrassment. Here's seven pounds. Release it and the money's yours."

"Absolutely not," said Manawydan.

"Ah, you drive a hard bargain," said the bishop. "Twenty-four pounds, then. It's ready money. I have it with me."

"I'll not hear of it," said Manawydan.

"Surely we can make some kind of deal," said the bishop. "Look here. You can have all my belongings. I'll give you my seven loads of baggage and the seven horses carrying them."

Manawydan could hardly believe his ears. Why was the bishop offering all his belongings to save a mouse's life? Could he be joking? Surely a man of God wouldn't play a trick on him.

"Keep your things," said Manawydan. "I'll not let the mouse go."

"What do you want then?" asked the bishop. "Name your price. I'll give you anything you want."

Before he could even think, Manawydan said, "I want Rhiannon and Pryderi freed."

"You shall have it," said the bishop.

Manawydan gasped with disbelief. Was the bishop the sorcerer who had caused Dyfed so much trouble?

"Do we have a deal?" asked the bishop.

"Not yet," said Manawydan. "I want something more."

"And what might that be?" asked the bishop.

"I want your magic and spells removed from all of Dyfed," said Manawydan.

"Consider it done," said the bishop. "Now please, hand me the mouse."

"Not yet," said Manawydan. "First I want to know who this mouse is."

"She's my wife," said the bishop.

"Your wife?" asked Manawydan with amazement.

"Of course," said the bishop. "Do you think I'd offer all my belongings to ransom a common field mouse?"

"But why did she steal from me?" demanded Manawydan. "And why have you put such a terrible spell on my home and my friends?"

"This will take some explaining," sighed the bishop. "You see, I'm not really a bishop. My name is Llwyd.[17] And I'm, as you must realize, a sorcerer. My quarrel wasn't with you, but with your friend Pryderi."

"What quarrel is this?" asked Manawydan.

"He did wrong to a friend of mine, many years ago," explained Llwyd. "The business doesn't really concern you. I sought to punish him by putting him under a spell and hurting all his loved ones.

"The people I rule wanted to take part in my revenge," continued Llwyd. "So I changed them to mice so they could destroy your wheat. On the third night, my pregnant wife joined the raiding party.

"If she hadn't been so large with child, you would never have caught her. And if you hadn't caught her, I would have plagued Dyfed forever.

"But now you've caught her, and I must pay the ransom you ask. I shall give Pryderi and Rhiannon back to you. And I shall remove the spell from Dyfed. So now, release her."

"Not yet," said Manawydan.

"What else do you want?" asked Llwyd.

"I want your promise to cast no more spells on this

[17](loid)

kingdom," said Manawydan.

"I promise," said Llwyd. "Now let her go."

"No," said Manawydan. "I need one more promise."

"What do you want now?" demanded Llwyd impatiently.

"You must give up taking revenge on Pryderi," insisted Manawydan. "You must never hurt him or his loved ones again."

Llwyd smiled. "Wisely asked, Manawydan," he said. "It's a good thing you brought that up. If you hadn't, I would've brought more harm to all of you."

"I thought as much," said Manawydan. "So do you promise?"

"I promise," said Llwyd. "Now set my wife free."

"Not until I see Pryderi and Rhiannon here beside me."

As quickly as he had asked, Pryderi and Rhiannon magically appeared. They blinked and shook their heads as if waking from a dream. Manawydan greeted his friend and wife with great happiness.

"Let my wife go now," said Llwyd.

"I'll do so gladly," said Manawydan as he untied the noose around the mouse's neck.

When Manawydan let the mouse go, the creature ran to Llwyd. Then the sorcerer touched her with a magic wand, and the mouse became a beautiful woman.

"Now look around your land," said Llwyd. "You'll see that I have kept the rest of my promises."

With those words, Llwyd and his wife disappeared. Manawydan and his friends looked around themselves in wonder.

All the missing homes were back where they belonged. All the farm animals had returned as well. And all the vanished people were going happily about their lives, as if nothing had ever happened.

Cigfa ran from the castle, her face beaming with delight. The four friends embraced each other with laughter and tears of joy. Then they returned to the castle Arberth. All was well in Dyfed once again.

INSIGHTS

This myth is part of a collection of Welsh tales called the *Mabinogion.* The Mabinogion is divided into four branches or parts. The tale of Manawydan is the third branch of the collection.

No one knows where the name Mabinogion came from. However, *mab* is the Welsh word for "son" or "boy," so it was thought that the tales had something to do with youth, either for teaching boys or to use as model tales for future storytellers.

Another theory is that Mabinogion originally meant "the collective material about the god Maponos." Maponos was a British god associated with hunting and music.

The myths in the Mabinogion are some of the oldest in Europe. They reach back to a time when the Celtic culture still dominated the British Isles. However, the stories were handed down by storytellers. It wasn't until the 11th century that a Christian monk wrote the tales down. That would explain the existence of Christian elements, such as the priest and bishop at the end of "Manawydan."

Poets held high positions in Celtic society. The Celtic poets were called bards, and they were believed to possess great wisdom. Legend has it that one poet by the name of Taliesin was able to change shape and travel outside his body. In fact, Taliesin was the perfect druid—that is, he knew all things of the past, present, and future. His spirit is said to live on in all the great poets of Wales.

Poetry is still important in Welsh society. Once a year, a national poetry festival called Eisteddfod is held. During the festival, people recite poetry in the Welsh language. This national celebration is repeated all over

continued

Wales, for the writing and reading of poetry is one of the favorite national pastimes.

The myth of Manawydan features Llwyd, a sorcerer. Sorcerers or wizards seem to be an integral part of the Welsh imagination. In fact, there are many places named after wizards of old.

There is a town in Wales said to be named after Merlin, the wizard made famous in the stories of King Arthur. Indeed, in this town there once grew an oak tree called Merlin's Oak. If the tree were ever destroyed, so the legend went, a great calamity would destroy the town. So even though the oak died, the people held the tree together with iron clamps and concrete. The tree was finally removed to make way for a street. To date, no reports of a calamity have been received.

Some scholars believe that the Celtic mythology of Wales is the original source of the King Arthur tales. Indeed, there are several similarities between the myth of Manawydan and the Arthur material.

For example, the golden basin to which Pryderi and Rhiannon become attached resembles the Holy Grail of King Arthur's legends. And the transformation of bountiful Dyfed into a gray wasteland is repeated in the tale of the Holy Grail. These likenesses suggest that both Welsh and British mythology have similar ancient roots.

THE DEATH OF KING ARTHUR

VOCABULARY PREVIEW

Below is a list of words that appear in the story. Read the list and get to know the words before you read the story.

attended (by)—taken care of; assisted; waited on
beguiling—misleading; distracting
clamoring—demanding noisily; insisting
disheartened—discouraged; saddened
edict—judgment; verdict
esteem—value; worth
feigned—pretended; faked
inevitable—bound to happen; certain
kindle—excite; stir up
kinsmen—relatives
mortal—able to cause death; fatal
nobles—people of the upper class; aristocrats
pacify—calm; soothe
siege—attack
solemn—serious
steadfast—loyal; faithful
stipulations—terms of an agreement; requirements
usurp—take control; seize
vouch (for)—give a guarantee; promise
yielded—let go; gave up

Main Characters

Agravain—Sir Gawain's brother; knight of the Round Table

King Arthur—King of Britain

Bedivere—knight of the Round Table

Gaheris—younger brother of Gawain; knight of the Round Table

Gareth—younger brother of Gawain; knight of the Round Table

Gawain—King Arthur's nephew; knight of the Round Table

Guinevere—King Arthur's wife; Sir Lancelot's lover

Lancelot—Guinevere's lover; knight of the Round Table

Mordred—King Arthur's son; knight of the Round Table

The Scene

The story takes place at Camelot, King Arthur's kingdom in England, and at Lancelot's castle in France.

The Death of King Arthur

There are times and places when everything seems perfect, when the world seems a dream of paradise. Such was Camelot during King Arthur's reign. But human weakness will always destroy perfection. So the magic of Camelot came to a tragic end.

We should all be ashamed of ourselves!" exclaimed Sir Agravain.[1] "Will none of us admit the truth? Sir Lancelot[2] is with Queen Guinevere[3] day and night. Anyone can see that they are lovers."

"Be quiet!" Agravain's older brother Sir Gawain[4] hissed back at him. "This is neither the time nor the place to speak of such things. Why, the king isn't even here. If you want to talk about this business, speak to him privately. Don't make it a public matter."

Indeed, Agravain had spoken his words very loudly. All the other knights in King Arthur's great meeting room could hear him. They began to gather around to listen to the angry knight.

"Well, I want to hear what Agravain has to say," said Sir Mordred,[5] standing up so that he could be heard by all. "Aren't we all equals, we knights here in Camelot?"[6] he asked with a sneer in his voice. "Doesn't everyone

[1] (ag´ ra vān)
[2] (lan´ sə lot)
[3] (gwin´ ə vper)
[4] (ga´ wān)
[5] (mōr´ dred) Mordred was both the son and nephew of Arthur. He was the son of Arthur and Arthur's half sister Morgan le Fay.
[6] Camelot was King Arthur's legendary castle and the city surrounding it. Even in legend, Camelot was not the capital of Britain. London was the capital, as it is today.

among us have a right to speak his mind?"

"You only want to stir up trouble," said Gawain to Mordred. "And I will not listen to such talk."

"Whether you listen or not, it's still the truth," exclaimed Mordred. Several knights shook their heads in agreement with Mordred's words.

"No good will come of this," said Gawain to Agravain and Mordred. "You'll divide our knights into those who support Lancelot and those who support King Arthur."

"Spoken like a friend of Lancelot," snapped Sir Agravain.

"Yes, I'm Lancelot's friend," replied Gawain. "And I'm the king's friend too."

"You can't be both," said Agravain. "If you're Lancelot's friend, you're a traitor, like him."

"Lancelot's no traitor!"

By this time all the knights were quarreling hotly. They surrounded Gawain and Agravain, taking sides with one or the other. Some urged Agravain to speak openly of the affair between the queen and Lancelot. Others agreed with Gawain that the matter should be forgotten.

"You suggested that I talk directly to the king about this," said Agravain, his eyes blazing. "Very well. As soon as he arrives, I'll do it."

"And I'll help you," said Mordred.

Gawain stood up. "I will not take part in any of this," he said angrily. "I would sooner die than sadden King Arthur."

With these words, Gawain walked out of the hall—his followers close behind him.

And just as Gawain and his followers left, a noble yet **solemn** man entered. The man was the ruler of all Britain—King Arthur. At the height of his powers, he had ruled much of Europe as well.

Arthur had come to the throne when he was just a boy. He had surprised all of Britain by withdrawing an enchanted sword from a stone. That sword had been thrust into the stone by the long-dead King Uther.[7] Uther

---

[7] (ū´ ther)

had ordered that whoever could remove the sword would be Britain's next king.

Many knights and **nobles** of Britain tried to pull the sword from the stone. They all failed. Meanwhile, Britain remained without a king.

One day, while passing the sword in the stone, Arthur decided to try to pull it out. To his surprise, the sword **yielded** easily to his touch.

You see, unknown to anyone but Merlin the Magician,[8] young Arthur was King Uther's son and the rightful heir to the throne. But to all the knights of Britain, Arthur was the younger son of a minor nobleman. After Merlin explained young Arthur's true identity, the boy was crowned king of Britain.

And Arthur proved to be the finest king Britain ever had. He drove Britain's enemies out of the country, and he slew monsters and destroyed dragons. But his finest act was to create the Fellowship of the Round Table.

He gathered 150 of the world's worthiest knights together to form this famous fellowship. At the Round Table, all knights shared their wisdom and power equally. As a result, King Arthur brought a golden age[9] to Britain.

But the knights of the Round Table had grown quarrelsome over the years. And the man who now entered the hall was not the mighty Arthur of years past. No, this man was aging and tired and growing **disheartened** with his rule.

"My lord, we have an urgent matter to discuss with you," said Sir Agravain.

"What is it?" asked King Arthur.

"It's Queen Guinevere and Sir Lancelot," replied Sir Agravain. "They are traitors to Britain. They are lovers."

King Arthur sighed sadly. This was not news to him. But he had hoped it would not become a matter for gossip among his knights.

---

[8] Merlin the Magician was King Arthur's protector and teacher.
[9] The golden age is a mythical period of perfect life on earth. Most of the world's cultures have a myth about a golden age. The British version is King Arthur's Camelot.

Queen Guinevere, with her long hair and sparkling gray eyes, was the most splendid queen in all the world. She was also a powerful queen, quite able to command whole armies. But she always used this power to serve her king with complete loyalty. Arthur loved her dearly.

Sir Lancelot was the son of the king of Benwick in France. Of all King Arthur's knights, Lancelot was the bravest and most loyal. He was Arthur's dearest friend.

In his heart, Arthur forgave Lancelot and Guinevere for falling in love. This was their only weakness. In all other ways, they were the most **steadfast** companions he could ever ask for. Because of this, Arthur chose to ignore their affair. He had hoped the other knights would do the same.

But now the knights were talking about it, and Arthur could ignore it no longer.

"This is a serious charge," King Arthur said to Agravain and Mordred. "How do you intend to prove it?"

"We'll settle it this way, my lord," explained Sir Mordred. "Tomorrow morning, announce that you are leaving the castle. Say that you plan to spend the night at your hunting lodge. Then go forth. Leave the rest to Sir Agravain and me."

"Sir Mordred and I will catch Sir Lancelot in the queen's bedroom," continued Sir Agravain. "When we do, we will bring him to you. Then you'll see him for the traitor he is."

"That will be no proof," said King Arthur to Sir Agravain. "You will have to prove Lancelot's guilt in heroic combat.[10] Are you prepared to do that?"

"I shall prove my loyalty, my lord," said Sir Agravain. "And I shall prove Sir Lancelot's guilt in the process."

The king reluctantly agreed to do as Mordred and Agravain suggested. The next morning, he left Camelot for his hunting lodge after announcing to everyone that he would be gone all night.

---

[10]In medieval tradition, guilt or innocence could be proven in combat. In defeat, a knight proved himself guilty; in victory, he proved himself innocent.

That evening, Agravain and Mordred, with twelve other knights, hid in a hallway near Queen Guinevere's bedroom. They hadn't waited long when they saw Lancelot enter the bedroom.

"Now we have him right where we want him," said Mordred with a sneer. "We'll let them get comfortable, then...."

The two lovers hadn't been alone in the room very long when there came a great pounding at the door.

"Sir Lancelot, we know you're in there," shouted Sir Agravain from outside the room. "Come out at once. You're a traitor to Britain. Face your trial in combat."

Lancelot carefully approached the door. He could hear the rattle of armor outside. He knew there were many knights awaiting him. Guinevere fearfully clung to Lancelot.

"Don't go!" she whispered. "You have no armor. You only have your sword. You'll surely be killed."

"I will die only if I am the traitor they say I am," said Sir Lancelot to Guinevere firmly. "If I *am* a traitor, let me die at their hands."

Lancelot let the door open just a little. One knight rushed into the room, and Lancelot bolted the door shut again. Even though Lancelot had no armor, he killed the knight easily. Meanwhile the other knights were pounding on the door, demanding entry.

Lancelot removed the dead knight's armor and put it on. Then he opened the door just a crack again. This time, Sir Agravain rushed into the room. Again Lancelot bolted the door behind him.

"So I stand face to face with my accuser," said Sir Lancelot.

"Only for a moment," snarled Sir Agravain. "Prepare to die, traitor."

Lancelot and Sir Agravain fought fiercely. But in a few moments, Agravain lay dead on the floor.

"Open the door, traitor," came the call of the other knights in the hall.

"Please go home," pleaded Lancelot with anguish in his voice. "I don't want to kill all of you."

"You won't have to worry about that," came the reply of one of the knights. "We'll see to it that it is you who dies tonight."

Reluctantly, Lancelot threw open the door. Before long the bodies of thirteen knights lay dead at Lancelot's feet.

The last knight to enter the room was Sir Mordred. He was shivering with fear. It seems that he was more skilled at hatching plans than fighting. He had waited outside while all the other knights fought Lancelot. In this way, he hoped to avoid fighting. But now he had no choice.

Mordred approached Lancelot timidly. Out of pity, Lancelot struck a glancing blow to Mordred's arm. With a cry of pain, Mordred rushed out of the room. He dared not stay and be killed like all his companions.

Lancelot and Guinevere stood staring in horror at the thirteen dead knights.

"What have I done?" exclaimed Lancelot miserably.

"You defended yourself," said Guinevere. "Were you supposed to stand and let them kill you?"

"But these knights were my friends and fellows!" cried Lancelot. "I've made myself exactly what they called me—a traitor to my king."

"You're no traitor," cried Guinevere.

"What else can you call a man who kills thirteen of his king's best knights? No, my dear. I am now Arthur's enemy, whether I wish to be or not. I must leave his kingdom before I bring more harm to him. And you must come with me."

"Oh, Lancelot, I cannot go," she said with tears forming in her eyes.

"But if you stay here, you'll be burned at the stake,"[11] Lancelot pleaded.

"You stood your ground bravely and risked your life,"

[11]In medieval times, a woman convicted of adultery could be burned at the stake.

said Guinevere. "Now I must do the same. Don't you see? Arthur is my king and husband. If I leave him now, I'll truly betray him. But if I am to be burned at the stake, come rescue me."

"I won't let them kill you," said Lancelot. "I'll come back for you."

Lancelot kissed Guinevere and fled into the night.

In the meantime, Mordred rushed on through the forest. He clutched his wounded arm and screamed with pain and fury. At last he reached King Arthur's hunting lodge and pounded on the door.

"What's happened to you, Mordred?" asked the king.

"I've been wounded by that villain Lancelot!" cried Mordred. "We found him in your wife's bedroom, just as we expected. Then he killed thirteen of your knights— including Sir Agravain! So there you are. What more proof do you need that Lancelot and Guinevere are guilty?"

"But doesn't Lancelot's success prove his innocence?" asked Arthur.

Mordred only scowled and remained silent.

The king's thoughts were filled with confusion and sorrow as he rode with Mordred back to Camelot.

"This is all so strange," Arthur thought to himself. "Perhaps Sir Lancelot has wronged me with his deeds. But in his heart, he is innocent and loyal. He proved it in combat by defeating Sir Agravain and the other knights. But the death of these fine knights will only **kindle** the anger of Mordred's followers. My worst fears have come true. The Fellowship of the Round Table is coming to an end.

"Well, no golden age can ever last forever," Arthur realized. "Human weakness will always bring a perfect time to an end."

When Arthur and Mordred arrived at the palace the next morning, angry knights surrounded the king.

"Sir Lancelot has escaped," some of them said. "But we have the queen. She's a traitor too. She must be put to death as soon as possible. We must burn her at the stake."

A few of the knights disagreed. They thought it would be wrong to act so rashly. Sir Gawain was among them.

"Doesn't chivalry[12] tell us we should be forgiving?" asked Gawain. "Why, the queen and Lancelot are not our enemies. Whatever wrongs they've committed, their hearts are true to their king. That's more than I can say for some among us."

"I'm surprised to hear you speak this way, Sir Gawain," remarked King Arthur. "Last night Lancelot killed two of your sons and your brother Sir Agravain. And your half-brother, Sir Mordred, was wounded as well. I would expect you to be the first calling for revenge."

"I wish my **kinsmen** were not dead," Gawain answered. "But I warned them not to get mixed up in this. They brought their deaths upon themselves."

King Arthur gathered the knights and listened to their arguments. As much as he wanted to agree with Gawain, honor required otherwise. He would have to break off his friendship with Lancelot forever. And he would have to sentence Queen Guinevere to death.

"Tomorrow morning," Arthur said, his voice choking with sadness, "the queen will be burned at the stake."

Gawain was deeply troubled by the king's **edict.** But he respected the king and would never speak against him. He decided to remain in his room and take no part in whatever happened next.

Arthur ordered Gawain's youngest brothers—Sir Gaheris and Sir Gareth[13]—to carry out the queen's execution. Like Gawain, they were unhappy that the queen had to die. But they were good knights and would not disobey their king.

---

[12]Chivalry was the code by which knights conducted themselves during the Middle Ages (A.D. 400-1400). According to the rules of chivalry, knights were expected to be brave, religious, generous, and polite. They were also expected to protect the weak.

[13](gā´ her is) (gār´ eth)

"We will obey your orders," Gareth told the king.

"But we will not carry weapons," Gaheris added. "If anyone should try to rescue her, we shall not be able to fight."

The king agreed. He more than half hoped someone would save his queen.

So when Gareth and Gaheris led Guinevere to the stake, they were unarmed. They tied the queen to a wooden post. Then each of them lowered a torch to the pile of wood under her feet. But before the wood could catch fire, trumpets sounded from outside the castle.

Gareth and Gaheris looked up with surprise. Sir Lancelot came riding through the castle gates, followed by many knights. King Arthur's knights stood guard around the queen at the stake. Lancelot broke through the guards, killing several as he approached the queen. In the confusion, he also killed Gareth and Gaheris.

Then Lancelot untied Queen Guinevere and carried her away. He had no idea he had killed Sir Gawain's beloved brothers.

As he had promised, Sir Gawain stayed in his room. Suddenly the silence of his chamber was broken by a knock at the door. It was King Arthur himself bearing awful news.

"My brothers, dead?" cried Sir Gawain.

"It's terrible but true," replied King Arthur.

"But why?" said Sir Gawain. "My brothers were unarmed. Why did Lancelot kill them?"

"I saw it happen," explained the king. "The knights around your brother were all armed and fighting. There was terrible confusion. Lancelot didn't know your brothers were unarmed. He was fond of both of them and would not have killed them on purpose."

"But he *did* kill them!" Sir Gawain cried out furiously. "Five of my kinsmen are now dead by Lancelot's hand. This is my thanks for taking his part! My king and uncle, I make you this sacred promise. Sir Lancelot is my enemy, now and forever. I will never make peace with him again.

And I shall not rest until I have met him in battle and one of us is dead!"

Sir Lancelot had a castle in Britain named Joyous Gard. It was there that he fled with Guinevere after he saved her. But as soon as he arrived, he began to prepare for the **siege** he knew was coming.

Then one morning, King Arthur and Sir Gawain arrived at Joyous Gard with a huge army. They stopped just outside the gate. Lancelot stood atop the castle wall and shouted to them.

"Welcome to Joyous Gard. What brings you in the dress of war?" asked Lancelot.

"I have come to get back my queen," said King Arthur.

"And I have come to kill you with my own hands," said Sir Gawain.

"You shall both be disappointed, then," replied Lancelot. "I won't give back Guinevere as long as you intend to burn her at the stake. And I won't fight either of you. I will not raise a hand against my king or my finest friend."

"Noble warrior, I have always held you in the highest **esteem,**" said King Arthur. "But you have killed many of my knights and taken my wife from me by force. Can you call such deeds anything except betrayal? And have you left me any choice other than to make war against you?"

"My lord, I am still your loyal subject," said Sir Lancelot. "You know perfectly well that I have never wronged you in my heart. Haven't I already proven this in combat with your knights? And now must I fight you— my two best friends—to prove it again? No, I shall not do it.

"As for your queen, she is as loyal to you as I am," continued Lancelot. "I rescued her from a wrongful death. If I had not done so, I would have dishonored myself forever."

"Your words are false, Sir Lancelot," cried Sir Gawain. "And your deeds are not so fine as you claim. You killed two unarmed boys who loved you dearly."

"And I loved them as if they were my own brothers," replied Lancelot sadly. "But I swear to you, I didn't mean to kill them. Till the day I die, I shall regret their deaths. Can you ask any more of me, Sir Gawain? You were always the most forgiving knight of all. Can't you forgive me now?"

"The time for forgiveness is long over," replied Sir Gawain bitterly. "Surrender the queen and fight me to the death."

"I will return Queen Guinevere to you only if you **vouch** for her safety," said Sir Lancelot. "As for fighting you, Sir Gawain, you know I shall never do so."

King Arthur took Sir Gawain aside to discuss their situation.

"Put your fury aside," the king begged Sir Gawain. "Let's forgive both Guinevere and Lancelot. Lancelot will give me back my queen and return to his own country. Then we need fight no more."

But Sir Gawain was too angry to make peace. King Arthur knew he had no right to command one of his knights not to fight another. It looked like war was **inevitable.**

King Arthur's soldiers lined up in front of Joyous Gard. Then, with a sad gesture from Arthur, they began to fire their arrows into the castle. Sir Lancelot sent his common soldiers out to fight with King Arthur's men. As for himself and his knights, they refused to join the fight. They stood on the castle walls, their arms crossed, bravely showing their refusal.

At one point, King Arthur was separated from his troops. One of Lancelot's men knocked the king from his horse and was about to kill him. Sir Lancelot called out and stopped his own soldier's hand. Then Lancelot made his way to the field and helped Arthur back onto his horse.

"This proves how wrong we were to fight," Arthur moaned to himself as he rode away. "Sir Lancelot is still my noblest and most loyal knight. Why must I treat him as my enemy?"

Forty knights were killed in the battle that day. The fighting continued during the days and nights that followed.

News of the war in Britain traveled far and wide. Finally word of the fighting reached the pope in Rome.[14] The pope sent a written order to stop the fighting at once. "Peace must be restored," the pope commanded. "Sir Lancelot must return Guinevere, and King Arthur must guarantee her safety."

Even the bold Sir Gawain dared not disobey the pope. He had no choice but to accept this peace, at least for the time being.

At the news of peace, Sir Lancelot opened his castle gates and allowed King Arthur and his knights to enter. Queen Guinevere came forward, dressed in her royal robes. Everyone present was stunned by her beauty.

"I am reluctant to let you go, my lady," said Sir Lancelot as he took her by the hand.

"My lord has promised my safety," replied Guinevere. "You may rely on his word."

"Be it so, then," said Sir Lancelot. "But if anyone in the kingdom so much as breathes a word against you, make sure I know it. I shall return and defend you."

Everyone present was deeply touched by Lancelot's loyalty to the queen. Then Lancelot let go of Guinevere's hand. She returned to the arms of her king, who lifted her onto a horse.

But then Sir Gawain stepped forward and spoke bitter words to Lancelot.

"Because the pope commands it, we will spare Guinevere's life," Sir Gawain said. "We will even give you

---

[14]The pope was the head of all Christians in Europe.

safe passage home to France. But you and I are not finished with our business. This peace is only for today. We
will do battle again, and one of us must die at the other's
hand."

Sir Gawain turned away. Then King Arthur, his
queen, and all his knights rode away from Joyous Gard
and returned to Camelot.

Lancelot and the knights loyal to him crossed the
channel[15] and made their way to Lancelot's castle in
France.

The war was ended, at least for now. But all was not
well in Camelot. King Arthur's heart was full of sorrow.
He could see that his Fellowship of the Round Table was
almost destroyed. The love and friendship among his
knights had vanished.

"It will be as if my golden age never existed," Arthur
thought. "It will be as if Camelot never was."

As Arthur feared, Sir Gawain kept **clamoring** for war.
He demanded that the king prepare a large army and
attack Lancelot's castle in France. Arthur knew that there
was no way to keep Gawain from waging war against
Lancelot. At last the king gave in to Gawain's demands.
He figured that if he went with Gawain, he might prevent
more bloodshed.

So King Arthur readied an army. Unwisely, the king
appointed Sir Mordred to rule England while he was
gone.

Arthur's army reached Benwick in France. They
fought hard against Lancelot's soldiers. As before, neither
Lancelot nor his knights took part in the battle. He
remained inside his castle, still refusing to raise a hand
against King Arthur or Sir Gawain.

For six months the fighting raged. The losses were
great on both sides, and neither army came near victory.

[15]The English Channel is a body of water separating England and France.

Then early one morning, Sir Gawain rode up to the gates of Benwick.

"When will you come out, Lancelot?" Sir Gawain called. "You have already proven yourself a traitor, many times over. Do you mean to prove yourself a coward as well?"

Lancelot heard Gawain's words with deep sadness. He knew he could stay out of the fighting no longer. He couldn't let more of his men die in his place. Honor required that he meet Gawain in combat.

So Lancelot put on his armor, took up his lance, and mounted his horse. He rode out of his castle, where he found Gawain ready and waiting for a joust.[16] Lancelot and Gawain each told their knights not to come to their aid. The warriors were to fight man-to-man until one of them yielded or died.

The two knights galloped their horses toward one another. With a mighty jolt, both lances shivered to pieces, but neither warrior was hurt. Then they attacked each other with their swords until their horses fell to the ground. Then the knights got to their feet, took up their swords, and kept on fighting.

They fought on into the morning. Lancelot was alarmed to find that Gawain didn't grow tired from the fighting. Instead, he seemed to grow stronger and more fierce.

Lancelot didn't know Gawain's secret. Long ago a magician had given Gawain a special power. From nine o'clock in the morning until noon, Gawain's strength increased three times. So as the morning wore on, Gawain grew stronger and stronger until he was three times stronger than the most powerful men. All this while, Lancelot grew more tired and weak.

But Lancelot was careful to save some of his strength. Again and again, he skillfully escaped Gawain's swinging blade. At last noon came and went, and Gawain's

[16]A joust was a form of medieval combat. In it, two mounted knights would try to strike each other down with lances—long, spear-shaped weapons.

strength returned to normal.

Lancelot felt the difference right away. He knew that he could now beat his opponent. Lancelot struck a powerful blow to Gawain's head, knocking off Gawain's helmet and sending him reeling to the ground. The ground was stained with Gawain's flowing blood. Lancelot stepped back.

"Why don't you kill me now?" Gawain demanded, unable to rise to his feet. "If you don't finish me off, I'll fight you again."

"Would you have me strike when you're down?" said Lancelot. "Yes, I suppose you would like it that way. It would prove me to be the coward you say I am. No, my friend. I won't give you that satisfaction."

And with those words, Lancelot retreated into his castle. Gawain had to be carried back to his tent. He lay there for three weeks, recovering from his wounds but not from his rage. One morning, when he had barely healed, he returned to Lancelot's castle.

"Come out and fight, traitor," Gawain called.

Lancelot appeared at the top of the castle wall.

"Why have you come back?" Lancelot called back. "I spared your life once and have no desire to fight you now. Can't we call our business finished?"

"I told you last time that you should have killed me," replied Gawain furiously. "Perhaps this time you'll think better of letting me go. I, for one, shall not rest until one of us is dead."

Lancelot rode out to fight Sir Gawain again. It was midmorning, and Gawain's strength was at its peak. But Lancelot had learned his lesson last time. He saved his strength and dodged Gawain's blows through the rest of the morning.

Then noon passed, and Gawain's strength returned to normal. As he had before, Lancelot struck a terrible blow to Gawain's head. Gawain's old wound was reopened, and he could not rise to his feet.

"Finish it," gasped Gawain.

"No," retorted Lancelot.

"Finish it now, or I'll be back again."

"Come back, then," said Lancelot. "We'll act out this little play a hundred times, if need be. I'd never strike a helpless enemy, much less my friend."

Again Lancelot returned to his castle. And again Gawain lay in his tent, recovering from his wounds. He healed more slowly this time. Night and day he prayed for enough health and strength to fight Lancelot again.

But he never got that chance. Before Gawain had fully recovered, King Arthur received terrible news from Britain—Sir Mordred had taken over the throne.

Mordred had planned quite skillfully. He faked letters from France saying that Lancelot had killed King Arthur. Then he **feigned** sorrow as he read these letters to the knights who remained in Britain. While the country mourned King Arthur's supposed death, Mordred managed to get himself crowned king.

But as always, Mordred wanted more. He wanted to marry Guinevere and make her his queen. Guinevere had seen through Mordred's schemes right from the start. She was quite sure King Arthur was not dead, and had no desire to become Mordred's wife. But cleverly, she pretended to accept Mordred's marriage proposal. Through her **beguiling** charms, Guinevere soon had Mordred fooled.

"My lord," she told him sweetly one day, "I have a great deal to do to prepare for the wedding."

"Such as?" asked Mordred.

"Well, there's not a single good dressmaker here in Camelot," Guinevere explained. "I'll have to go to London for a wedding gown—that is, if you want me to look my best."

Mordred was delighted by Guinevere's desire to look good for him. So foolishly, he let her go to London, **attended** by ladies and knights loyal to her. Once there Guinevere gathered food, clothing, and weapons. Then she and her followers locked themselves in the Tower of

London[17] and refused to come out.

When Mordred heard what the queen had done, he was furious. But he knew better than to let Guinevere see his anger. He went to London and stood in front of the Tower. Then he tried to **pacify** her with charming words.

"My sweet, perhaps I rushed you too much," he said pleasantly. "We don't have to be married right away. Why don't we wait a week or two? Or perhaps a month?"

"So you can **usurp** my husband's place along with his throne? Never!" Guinevere shouted back. "I'd rather die than marry you!"

Angrily, Mordred returned to Camelot, where he was greeted with grim news. An army was crossing the channel from France. Of course, Mordred knew it was Arthur.

Mordred wasted no time gathering his forces. His knights rode straight to Dover[18] and waited for the arrival of the attacking army. The battle began in the early morning hours. Mordred's soldiers sailed out in boats to meet the attackers. Soon the waves breaking on the British shore were red with British blood.

Arthur's troops were outnumbered, but their hearts were loyal to their king. And Arthur himself, though old, was still a mighty warrior. He fought bravely.

Gawain, however, was struck a deadly blow, which opened his head wound again. Knowing he was dying, Gawain made his way to King Arthur.

"I am dying at Lancelot's hand, after all," Sir Gawain told his king. "Lancelot—your noblest knight—has truly proven his innocence. And my own stubbornness and anger has finished me. Worse, I set you and Lancelot against one another. I did more than my share to bring about Camelot's fall. I pray you now, make peace with Lancelot."

With his few remaining breaths, Sir Gawain asked the

[17] The Tower of London is an ancient fortress, often used throughout history as a prison.

[18] Dover is a city on the southern coast of England overlooking the Strait of Dover. Dover, famous for its tall, white cliffs, is only twenty miles from France.

king for pen and paper. Gawain then wrote a letter to Lancelot in which he begged for Lancelot's forgiveness. Then, just at the hour of noon, Sir Gawain died.

King Arthur regrouped his army and marched against Mordred. Once Mordred's knights recognized Arthur, they joined their true king as he marched toward Camelot. Fresh volunteers flocked to Arthur's side.

King Arthur and his army reached the forests near Camelot the next evening. Arthur planned to attack Mordred in the morning. So his army set up camp to await the dawn. But that night King Arthur had a strange dream.

He dreamed he was sitting on a throne placed on a platform high above the earth. He was wearing his crown and his gold robes. Below him, serpents, dragons, and wild beasts were swimming in the murky waters of a well. Suddenly the platform tilted, and Arthur was flung down into the water. The monsters attacked him.

Arthur cried out in his sleep, but he didn't wake up. Still in his dream, he found himself standing face to face with the ghost of Sir Gawain.

"My lord and uncle," said Gawain, "I bring you this dream as a warning. If you fight Mordred tomorrow, you shall not fare well. Many of your knights shall die, and so shall you."

"But what shall I do?" asked King Arthur.

"Delay the battle," answered Gawain.

"For how long?"

"One month," explained Gawain. "By then, Lancelot shall have received my letter. He shall arrive with his own knights. Together, you and he shall defeat Mordred. For now, farewell. Forgive me for all the trouble I have brought you."

King Arthur's eyes snapped open. He was awake in his tent and deeply troubled by his dream. He called his knights together and told them what he had learned. Everyone agreed that the battle should be postponed for one month as Gawain's ghost suggested.

King Arthur sent two men to Mordred to arrange a truce. These were Sir Lucas and Sir Bedivere. They found Sir Mordred in command of a tremendous army. Mordred was unwilling to make peace easily. He bargained and argued with Lucas and Bedivere, insisting on his own terms. At last Mordred agreed to a truce, but only if certain **stipulations** were met.

King Arthur was to grant him rule over Cornwall and Kent right away.[19] Also, Mordred was to become king of all Britain when King Arthur died. Lucas and Bedivere returned to Arthur and told him Mordred's terms. King Arthur knew he had no choice but to accept.

The next day King Arthur and Mordred met in an open field to sign the truce. Each of them was guarded by fourteen knights. Both of their armies stood and watched at a distance.

Suspicion filled the air, and the knights were heavily armed. All were under orders to keep the peace. But if any knight saw an enemy sword unsheathed, the order was to attack.

All was silent as Mordred and Arthur signed the treaty. At last the truce seemed certain. Arthur and Mordred each raised a glass of wine in a toast. But a snake slithered unnoticed from the underbrush. It coiled about the leg of one of the knights and bit him. Before the knight could think, he had drawn his sword. In an instant, both armies rushed into deadly battle.

Two hundred thousand men died that day. Victory and defeat lost all meaning. The most noble knights in England were soon dead or dying. Arthur stood staring at the field of corpses in sorrow and despair. Then he saw Mordred standing among his own slain warriors.

"I will kill him now," Arthur whispered to himself. "I will kill him, even if it costs my life."

Arthur raised his spear and rushed at Mordred. Seeing the king coming, Mordred raised his sword and shield. In his fury, Arthur drove his spear through

[19]Cornwall and Kent are two counties in the southern part of England.

Mordred's shield and into Mordred's body.

Knowing he was about to die, Mordred painfully pulled himself forward along Arthur's spear. Then with his final ounce of strength, Mordred struck the king a **mortal** blow. Mordred's sword pierced Arthur's helmet and laid open his skull. Mordred then fell dead.

With the death of Mordred, a deep silence settled on the battle field. Loyal Sir Bedivere was the only knight left standing. While wandering the field, Bedivere found his dying king. In a deathly whisper, King Arthur began to give his last commands.

"Take my sword, Bedivere," he said. "Take it to the lake nearby and throw it far into the water. Then come back and tell me what you see."

As he was commanded, Bedivere took King Arthur's sword in his hands. He felt unworthy to hold such a weapon. But he walked straight to the water and prepared to throw the sword. But then he hesitated.

Bedivere sat down to gaze at the beauty of weapon. Arthur's sword was named Excalibur, and many stories were told about its power. It was said that King Arthur had received the sword from a mysterious Lady of the Lake.

"It seems a shame to throw such a marvelous weapon away," Bedivere said to himself. "I'll hide it, and the king will know no different."

So Bedivere hid the sword where he could find it again. Then he returned to his dying king's side.

"What did you see?" Arthur asked him.

"I threw the sword." was Bedivere's reply. "Then I saw the sword splash into the water. Nothing more."

"You lie," said Arthur with sadness in his eyes. "Return to the lake and follow my command—throw Excalibur into the water."

Again Bedivere could not force himself to part with the sword. When he returned to Arthur, he told the same story.

"I beg of you," was Arthur's plea. "Please fulfill my

wishes. I don't have much time."

Feeling the power of King Arthur's request, Bedivere vowed to overcome his desire for the sword. With all his might, he threw the sword as far as he could across the water. But before the sword fell into the lake, a woman's hand reached up out of the water. The hand caught the sword, waved it three times, then disappeared into the deep. Bedivere was breathless with wonder.

The knight returned to his dying king and told him what had happened. King Arthur fell back in relief. He was very near death now, and could barely speak. Summoning his strength, Arthur begged Bedivere to carry him to the lake.

When they reached the lake, a mysterious boat was waiting at its edge. Many beautiful ladies were in the boat, wearing black veils and weeping sadly.

"What must I do now, my lord?" asked Bedivere.

"Place me on the boat, good knight," gasped Arthur. "It shall take me to a valley called Avalon.[20] There my wounds shall be healed. If you never hear of me again, remember me in your prayers."

Bedivere did as he was ordered. The boat sailed off into the mists, and Arthur was never heard from again.

A month later, Sir Lancelot arrived in Britain, just as Sir Gawain's ghost had promised. Lancelot was stricken with grief to find that he had come too late. His king and all the finest knights in England were now dead.

Lancelot asked everyone he met where Guinevere had gone. At last he learned that she had gone into a convent.[21] She intended to become a nun and devote the rest of her life to helping the poor.

Lancelot went to the convent to speak to her one last time. But when Guinevere saw him, she turned her face away.

"Don't look at me," she said. "Our love has been the ruin of Britain. It has been the death of the finest king

---

[20]In some retellings, Avalon is described as a cave or an island.
[21]A convent is place where nuns live apart from the rest of society.

who ever lived. Now I only want to seek forgiveness for my sins. Go back to France and rule your kingdom well. Take a wife and live in happiness. As much as I love you, I want never to see you again."

"My queen," Lancelot replied, "if you would leave here, I would take you back to my kingdom to be my wife. But I will marry no one else. If you turn away from the world, I will do the same. But won't you kiss me one last time?"

"No," said Guinevere, simply and tearfully. "No."

True to his word, Lancelot disappeared into the woods. He built a little chapel and became a hermit. He spent the rest of his days alone, praying for forgiveness.

And what of King Arthur? Where is this mysterious valley called Avalon? No one knows. But some people still say that Arthur is resting there. And someday, when the time is right, he will return and rule Britain again.

INSIGHTS

King Arthur was probably a real person, though no one knows much about him. But there are several theories about who this real Arthur was.

One theory states that Arthur was a British king called Riothamus, who ruled in the 5th century. Riothamus—whose name means "high king"—is similar to the legendary Arthur in that he led an army of 12,000 into Gaul (France).

Probably the most popular theory is that the real Arthur was a Welsh cavalry general named Arturius. (The Welsh live in the southwestern part of England.) Between A.D. 500 and 517, Arturius led twelve successful attacks against the invading Saxons (Germanic tribes).

Arthur first appears as a major hero in the works of Geoffrey of Monmouth. Geoffrey wrote a book called *History of the Kings of Britain.* However, most scholars consider this a work of fiction, not history.

According to Geoffrey, Arthur conquered all of the British Isles and most of Europe. Geoffrey wrote that Arthur would have taken Rome too if he hadn't been called home to fight his nephew. (In later stories, it's Arthur's son who tries to take over the throne.)

Legends about Arthur grew as time passed. Soon the "real" Arthur was all but forgotten as the legendary man became more and more popular.

Sir Thomas Malory, who lived in 13th-century England, wrote another version of Arthur's deeds called *Le Morte D'Arthur.* (The title means "The Death of Arthur.")

The circumstances under which Malory wrote the

continued

book are rather interesting—he penned it while in prison.

Being in prison was a common experience for Malory. He was in trouble with the law all his life and was jailed eight times. Malory did manage to escape twice—once by swimming the prison moat and another time during an armed breakout.

What was Malory jailed for? His crimes were numerous. Once he tried to attack and murder a duke. He also broke into an abbey and robbed it. And he was charged at various times with highway robbery and cattle theft.

Yet somehow, between his prison escapes and criminal deeds, Malory did find time to write. And oddly enough, his account of the Arthur legend proved to be one of the most popular. Criminal though he was, Malory created wonderful portraits of nobles who lived by a strict code of honor.

Sources differ about the origin of Arthur's Round Table. According to some stories, Arthur had the table built so his knights would stop arguing about who had the best seat. Others say that Guinevere's father gave Arthur the table as a wedding gift.

Sources also disagree about how many knights the Round Table seated. Some sources say 150 men were able to fit around the table. Another insists that the table was big enough for 1,600 knights!

Characters in Northern European myths often share some similar—and sometimes amazing—qualities. In this story, for example, Gawain's strength increased till noon and lessened from then on. It is for this reason that he may have once been associated with a Celtic sun god.

Gawain's father was Loth. This name is similar to both the Welsh name Lleu and the Irish name Lugh. Both of these beings were sun gods.

Gawain also had many adventures like those of the Irish hero Cuchulain. And like Gawain, Cuchulain was the son of Lugh.

Infidelity in marriage was fairly common during the time of King Arthur. Marriage among the nobility was arranged by the couple's family. Or sometimes the ruling lord set up a match between people for political or economic reasons. As for divorce, it didn't even exist.

Since people didn't pick their own mates, it's not surprising that couples rarely loved each other when they married. So in search of love, husbands and wives often had affairs. In fact, affairs were so common, they were almost expected.

While affairs may have been commonplace, they were still regarded as sinful. During the legendary search for the Holy Grail, Lancelot's affair with Guinevere cost him dearly.

According to legend, the Holy Grail was the cup Christ drank from at the Last Supper before his death. All Arthur's knights were eager to find the cup. But a heavenly voice announced that Lancelot wasn't fit to claim it.

However, it was fated that Lancelot would play a crucial role in the quest. While he wasn't noble enough, his son Galahad was. Galahad not only found the Grail but was lifted straight to heaven when he discovered it.

According to this myth, Arthur never really died. Instead, he was taken away to a mythical valley (or cave or island) called Avalon.

But according to the legend, Arthur will return at England's greatest hour of need to save his country. This legend is reflected in the words on a tombstone in Glastonbury where Arthur is supposedly buried. The tomb reads, "Here lies Arthur, king that was, king that shall be."